◄EYE OF THE►
MOON

DIANNE HOFMEYR

D0589978

SIMON AND SCHUSTER

For David

SIMON AND SCHUSTER
First published in Great Britain in 2007
by Simon and Schuster UK Ltd
A CBS COMPANY

This paperback edition published in 2008

Simon & Schuster UK Ltd
Africa House, 64–78 Kingsway, London WC2B 6AH.

A CIP catalogue record for this book is
available from the British Library.

ISBN: 978-1-41691-068-8

Typeset by Rowland Phototypesetting Ltd,
Bury St Edmunds, Suffolk
Printed and bound by Cox & Wyman, Reading, Berkshire

www.simonsays.co.uk
www.diannehofmeyr.com

MOON. RULER OF THE STARS.
PROTECTOR OF WOMEN.
EYE OF WISDOM,
TRUTH AND SECRETS ...

Without two fingers, it's hard to grip a reed stylus. So I write this story with difficulty, sitting on the bank of the Great River far from the city of Thebes. Perhaps in time to come the words will be carved more accurately in stone and the truth known to all. Poison, slavery and murder – all are part of this story.

I am Isikara, daughter of the Priest and Embalmer at the Temple of the Crocodile God, Sobek. But first I should explain my injury.

The first two fingers are the bow fingers. Until my right hand was forced open against the ground, a cleaver raised and both fingers sliced through, I had not understood their importance. They are the ones that pluck the gut and send the arrow with purpose. Strength is crucial in pulling back the bowstring. But it's the final release of these fingers that controls the arrow and sets it on its path. Right to the heart of the enemy.

What better way to maim a bowman, than to take away the bow fingers?

Of the two of us, Anoukhet was the better marksman. She pulled the arrow back with the strength of someone twice her size and sent it on its way with the true eye of a hunter. Deadly accurate!

Side by side we stood. Side by side we were captured. Sisters in combat. But that's behind us now. I've put aside my arrow and bow and changed my boy's tunic for a robe more suited to a girl. Anoukhet has too. Yet a girl's robe doesn't prevent her from fieriness. And we both still carry daggers in our belts.

It might seem strange that a girl writes of plotting and warfare. But there are many things both strange and unusual ahead. Not least that I should be *able* to write. Few girls are scribes. But my father taught me well. Not only the art of forming words on papyrus with a reed stylus but also the art of writing in the new, flowing, hieratic, cursive style. It's quicker than hieroglyph and suits my impatience.

There's much to tell. My words flow fast ahead of me now and my reed blots the sooty ink and leaves behind dark smudges on the papyrus. The story grows so fast, that should I not be able to find enough soot and sap to mix more ink, I would write it in blood . . . even my own.

CHAPTER ONE

THE GREAT CROCODILE GOD ... SOBEK

There was a moment of absolute stillness just before my brother screamed. The sound tore through me. I can still hear it – the worst scream I've ever heard.

I ran down the path to the crocodile pit. He was clinging to the edge of the stone wall. A crocodile had hold of his arm and was wrenching and tossing its head, in a fury of movement and sound. Inside the pit, the other crocodiles were leaping and thrashing and snapping in their eagerness to get at him as well.

'Get the stick! The stick, Kara! Do something!' Katep bellowed. His eyes were glazed with terror.

I searched frantically. The forked crocodile stick that usually stood next to the wall wasn't there.

Nothing was in its place. I had no weapon. Not even a branch to shove between the iron grip of the beast's jaws, or poke at its eyes, or beat across its head.

I stood paralysed. I knew a crocodile's brutality. The sudden lashing out at an unsuspecting victim. The way they tossed their victims before dragging them below the water. One final thrust of its tail, one quick arch of its body, and it would throw my brother Katep high into the air and then catch him again in a stronger, more *fatal* grip. It would be too late then.

I spun around frantically and grabbed whatever I could. Sand and more sand. And flung it as hard as I could at those reptile eyes. Again and again, I sent a hailstorm of sand into the air.

Suddenly, with a wild angry snort, it shook its head viciously. Then lost its grip on my brother and sunk back below the wall into the pit. Katep fell limp to the ground at my feet, blood streaming from a limb so torn it no longer had the appearance of an arm.

There was so much blood I thought he would die. How could anyone live when there was so much blood everywhere?

But he didn't die.

*

The crocodiles were kept for sacrifice. Katep was responsible for feeding and caring for them. My father, High Priest at the Temple, makes sacred offerings of them to appease the Crocodile God, Sobek. At certain times of the moon the crocodiles are ritually washed, one is chosen, killed, and then embalmed.

My work is to help with embalming. To mix the resins and prepare the linen mummy wraps. Crocodiles are cumbersome and difficult to wrap. A method has to be followed so that the bindings cross over one another and make a woven pattern. Afterwards eyes and teeth are painted on the mummy.

That's the part I enjoy most – painting the ferocious eyes and terrible teeth. But I can never manage to make them as frightening in death as they are in life.

The mummified crocodiles are placed in special sacred vaults below the Temple to keep Sobek company. Row upon row of them lined up on the stone shelves like so many loaves of bread. Food for the gods.

But now, since Katep's accident, the job of caring for the crocodiles has fallen to me.

Katep's wound has healed to an angry stump but the healing of his heart has taken longer. He is restless, without direction, and refuses to speak of it. The accident has left him silent and resentful, with a burning anger that finds no outlet in action. Katep was a hunter. He could bring down wildfowl with the flick of his throwstick and stop any hare in mid-spring with his arrow. Without being able to hunt, Katep is no longer Katep.

'I'm leaving!' he announces one morning.

'Why?'

He shrugs impatiently. 'I have no place here. *Everything* I do requires the skill of both hands. I feel trapped. Helpless. I *have* to leave.'

I stare back at him. He knows I know that he is looking for the impossible. 'Where will you go?'

'I'm not sure.'

'So?'

He shrugs again. It seems his shoulders have forgotten there is only one arm to move.

'Perhaps to the desert camps of the camel-dealers in the Sudan. Or to the gold and amethyst workings in Nubia. Or the turquoise workings of Sinai.'

I eye him. He might as well have said he is leaving this earth and going into the Underworld.

'So far?' is all I say. His silence tells me he knows I'm really saying, How will you manage with only the

8

stump of an arm? 'I'll never see you again. Nubia and the Sudan and Sinai are all far beyond Egypt's borders. They're our *enemies!*'

He gives a fleeting smile, his face handsome, despite his anger. 'Egypt's enemies, not mine, Kara!' Then he shakes his head. 'I *can't* stay here. I don't want to be a priest or a stonemason as Father wants me to be.'

I kick the sand with my bare foot. 'Why not?' I ask, even though I understand his anger and frustration. Understand his determination to leave. I know he *will* go ... *has* to go ... no matter how much I plead.

He brandishes the stump of his arm. Beats the air with it. 'Have you heard of a stonemason cutting stone with something like this?'

The scars on the stump are still raw and red. Dreadful to look at. But at the same time, fascinating. I know each scar as well as the moles on my arm. I've cleaned them, smeared the wounds with unguents and bound them daily, ever since that day I had to hold him down while my father injected the arm with scorpion venom to numb it and cut away the shreds of flesh before stitching the skin together.

Now the scars make hieroglyphs across his flesh and tell their own story. I know Katep cannot bear to look at them. It's a burden for him to carry this stump around. No wonder he wants to shrink from it and run away. It's not me, or Father, that he's running from. It's his arm.

I know this in my head but my heart makes me speak out differently.

'Don't go! Please don't go! You can't go! You said we'd go away *together* one day. We made plans. Remember? In the fork of the mimosa tree, the day we watched the crocodiles laying eggs in the sand.'

He gives me a withering look. 'We were children then.'

I flick the side plaits of my wig back from my face and squint at him. Feel like a chastised child. 'Is that *all* your promise counts for?'

We had pricked our thumbs with mimosa thorns. I had put my thumb against his and mingled our blood. It was a blood vow. There hadn't been a need. Our blood is already bonded. We share the same thoughts and feel things in common. Between us there is a thread as fine and silvery as a spider's web. Invisible but just as strong. It is difficult to snap.

'Half the boat belongs to me!' is all I say. But he knows I'm thinking, Who will catch fish with me now? Or trap and roast frogs? Or dare me to walk along the wall of the crocodile pit?

He stares back at me. He has read my thoughts. 'Promise not to walk on the crocodile wall.'

I pull a face at him. 'Hah! You never worried about anything dangerous before! *You* were the one who dared me to enter the labyrinth the first time!'

'That was different. There were two of us. And don't go in there either, Isikara!'

Why is he calling me Isikara, instead of Kara? Already I am no longer his sister. I give him a hot look from between the strands of my hair. 'Don't leave me!'

'Then join me.'

I shake my head. 'By the white feather of Truth, you know I can't! I *cannot* break the vow I made to Mother on her death pallet. I promised I'd care for Father. Weave the linen. Be his Temple assistant. Help boil the resins for embalming. Look after his embalming tools.' I kick the sand again and swallow hard, fighting my tears with anger. 'Now I have to look after the crocodiles as well!'

'Don't trust them even if they look half asleep.'

'Hah! I don't need your advice!' I squint through the sunlight at him, daring him to change his mind.

'Kara, don't be so cross.' For a moment he forgets his own anger and grabs me around the neck with his good arm. I sense the other arm wanting to hold me as well. But the stump flounders, directionless in the air. Instead he puts on a deep, fierce voice, 'I am Sobek! I seize like a ravening beast!'

'Stop it! Don't mock Sobek!' I push him away so he won't see my tears. My hand flies to the moonstone amulet at my neck. Quickly I draw the Eye of Horus in the sand with my big toe to ward off the evil eye and keep Katep protected.

The morning he sails, I hand him a small linen bag to hang around his neck. Inside are the bodies of a dried lizard and a frog, and a lock of our mother's hair as well to keep him safe. I give him a sack of pomegranates and some shelled beans and two loaves with some potted meat of wildfowl. I had killed the bird myself with my throwstick. Then I hand him a small amulet of blue glass I'd bartered for in the marketplace.

'It's a scorpion. To ward off evil. Watch out for scorpions under the rocks of Sinai.'

'In Sinai, there are men employed as scorpion charmers.'

I eye him. He hasn't left yet, but already he knows things I don't know and something jabs at my heart

12

as sharp as the sting of a scorpion. 'But what if their charm doesn't work?'

He laughs. 'Stop worrying! The Scorpion Goddess, Seqet, will protect me!'

Then he sails down the silver ribbon of water that joins the Great River. I run along the mud bank trying to keep up with his boat. Perhaps I hope the burden of me running alongside will drag him back, like an anchor to the shore. But no – his boat travels lightly forward and my feet remain stuck to the bank.

'I'll never see you again!' I call after him. And say a quick, silent prayer to Hathor to beg that it won't be true.

'Of course you will.'

'Send me signs that you are safe. Sing songs and say incantations to keep the crocodiles and hippopotami away from the boat. Have you remembered your spear and your throwstick?'

To all this he nods and smiles back at me.

'And beware of crocodiles. If the boat lodges in reeds don't climb out into the water. Even if it is only up to your ankles!'

He laughs. 'Must I remain inside the boat for the rest of my life?'

'Just be careful, Katep!'

13

'Don't worry, I won't be caught again. I've already given Sobek my offering.' He grins. Then he tucks the sail rope under his chin so he can raise his left arm in a salute. He gives me a last look. Then he turns his back and begins paddling with his one good arm.

When I can't keep up with him any longer, I stand and watch his reed boat beat against the wind and the choppy waves. I touch the smooth cool moonstone of my amulet once more and feel for the knots on my plaited reed bracelet and call upon all that is evil to remain tied up and out of his reach.

I watch his back and the sail grow smaller and smaller until it is nothing but a moth skimming across the water to an unknown place. I blink and narrow my eyes against the breeze to prevent moisture being squeezed from them. A lump rises up in my throat like a bloated, angry toad.

It's said those who sail the Great River either look forward or look back. That morning when Katep left, he stood stiff-backed to everything he had left behind. I stared after him, willing him to turn around. But he didn't! Not once!

With that sail went my heart. I never thought Katep would take the boat and go without me. I stared after him and wished my own life would change. But wishing is dangerous. Wishes have a way of coming back to you.

The next morning I dragged a slaughtered goat by its horns to the crocodile pit. It was heavier than I thought and I cursed Katep for leaving me to do his work.

I could see by the swollen udder it was a she-goat. The goat's kid would be searching between the other goats now. Nosing for the full udder of its mother. But my father only believed in sacrificing she-goats to the crocodiles. Male goats were too precious, he said. They carried the seed of the future herd.

What about she-goats? Weren't they the true future of the herd? But my father was impatient with me and Katep's leaving made him more impatient than usual.

The goat was limp and heavy. My father had slit her throat and flies were already buzzing around the gash. The track left in the sand by her dragging hooves and body was spattered with drops of blood that glistened like red garnets. I was glad she was already dead. Offerings are usually made alive. But with Katep gone, I had begged my father to kill the goat first so I wouldn't have to listen to her bleating.

The nearer I got to the pit, the more my feet dragged and the tighter I clutched the forked stick.

The crocodiles were moving restlessly in their pit as they sensed the scent of the she-goat's blood and the warm, sweet smell of her milk. I heard their angry hisses and their tails hitting against the stone, and the sound of jaws snapping and clashing as they lashed at each other.

'Be careful of their tails!' Katep had warned.

I didn't need his reminder.

My father was distraught the morning he discovered Katep's empty bed. 'Why did he leave without bidding farewell? There was no need for him to go. He could've stayed and learned my profession. Assisted me in the Temple. Learned the art of embalming from me.'

I gave my father a dark look. 'Is my work not good enough? Am I not your assistant? Katep was never interested in learning to embalm. Besides, it's not his fault he had to leave. It's the fault of a crocodile!'

'Hush! Hold your tongue! To be chosen by the most sacred crocodile, Sobek, is the greatest honour.'

'I'd rather die without honour,' I snapped.

He shook his head. 'Kara! Kara! You're too

headstrong. It'll get you into trouble. You need a mother to groom you in ways suitable for women. You've too much to say for yourself. You must learn not to speak out. To think before you speak.'

'But—!'

'Enough!'

The day Katep lost his arm, my father inscribed above the portal of the crocodile pit: *To be devoured by the Crocodile God, Sobek, is to be possessed for ever by Divinity.*

But the words were more solace to my father than to Katep.

Now, as I passed under these words, shivery bumps came up on my arms. I had no desire to be eaten by a crocodile.

I understood my father's anger and hurt that Katep had left without saying farewell. We both missed him more than we could say. The house was quieter with him gone. When he left, something left with him. Our meals were taken in silence opposite his empty place, each with our thoughts far away.

Mine ran on to things other than the daily drudge of cooking, weaving linen, and feeding, watering and caring for crocodiles. They were wild and free. They were with Katep – with what he might be doing, and the river he was exploring, and the new things he would discover without me.

Suddenly, as I stood ready to heave the goat into the pit, I realised that with his going, Katep had snapped the thread between us – the thread that I'd thought could never be broken.

CHAPTER TWO

DAZZLING ATEN

I woke long before the water of the Great River stole blue from the sky. On the roof terrace, the stars were turning pale in the east. The chilly air brought goosebumps to my arms as I touched the moonstone of the amulet at my throat – three times for good luck – then felt for the seven knots tied in my plaited papyrus bangle and whispered the prayers that would invoke each knot to tie up any evil that might be lurking. My hands moved from amulet to knots without thinking. They were rituals done as easily as breathing or brushing a fly from my face.

The embers in the clay oven were still warm enough

to stir into life. I lay down two loaves that had been proving overnight and dragged the embers around them. Soon there was a smell of warm barley dough in the air. Then I crept downstairs, past my father's sleeping chamber and Katep's empty corner and stepped outside into the courtyard that was still shadowy and silent. Even the fish in the reflecting pool still slept. The air was heavy with the perfume of figs and ripening dates as I swept the entrance with a mimosa branch to ward off plagues from entering our home that day.

I took two leather buckets and strode down to the river to fetch my father's bathing water. The water-buffalo were moving restlessly in their byre, pushing and nosing each other in their eagerness to get at the fresh clumps of grass on the sedge islands. Their horns stood out like dark lyres against the pale sky.

Some mornings a warm desert wind played music on those lyres. A strange, enchanting song that came from a far-distant place. A sound that made my feet want to dance and swirl away over the sand dunes. Today there was no wind. Just the early chill that made the skin of the buckets stiff as I carried them down to the river's edge.

The floods were coming. Every day the water was pushing higher and the small islands were disappearing. Thoth, the God of Wisdom and Truth, was weighing sunshine and darkness. Soon the day would come when they would balance equally on his scales, and then sunshine would tip heavier.

Each morning as the light crept in from the east, I watched for a tiny sliver of the first moon. This morning it was floating just above the edge of the earth. A transparent shaving, as fine as a single thread of spun flax. I touched the moonstone amulet and invoked Hathor, Goddess of the Moon, Protector of Women, to protect me.

The first moon marked the day of Ritual, when the crocodiles were brought down to the stone pool in the river to be cleansed of evil. Today one would be selected as a sacrifice to Sobek and would be prevented from returning along the passageway that led back to the pit.

The water was smooth, silent and cold around my ankles. I watched for bubbles to make sure no wild river crocodile was lurking below the surface, and then I checked the stone wall of the pool for gaps. It was a bad omen to allow a sacred crocodile to escape.

But it was still too early to slide back the stone that opened the passageway. The crocodiles in the pit wouldn't stir themselves until they had been warmed by the sun. I'd purposely not fed them since giving them the she-goat. Getting them down to the water was easy. Getting them back to the pit was difficult. The village children had to bang cymbals and beat sticks against the walls to urge them on.

'Remember to leave a slaughtered goat in the pit,' Katep had instructed. 'One that's just beginning to rot! The smell of rotting meat brings them out of the water, like flies to a dung-heap!'

Now the sweet perfume of lotus lilies drifted across the water. The sun was just rising and drawing up the buds from beneath the water. As their blue petals opened to reveal a brilliant golden heart, it was like the sky being greeted by the sun. Each evening the lilies closed again and sank back into the dark water, trapping the scent of the golden heart between their petals.

I was first at the river. None of the other village girls had arrived yet. We teased that whoever was early enough would be greeted by the most handsome God of all – Nefertem, God of the Blue Lotus and God of the Sunrise, who brought the sun into the sky. He would rise from the river with a lotus on his head and carry the girl away on a body as powerful as a lion's.

We all longed to be the one chosen, but however early I came, I never saw him.

I filled my buckets and picked three lilies to perfume my father's bathing water, then squeezed the water from the edge of my wrap and turned to walk back. There was a smell of wood-smoke now and I could hear babies crying and dogs yapping and squabbling over bones at the rubbish heaps, and women singing as they went down the pathways to work on the land.

Suddenly there was a shout. I looked back. My breath caught as I saw a huge boat floating silently across the water. It was not the usual barge that collected tithes for the Temple granaries – the one that came piled with sacks of grain for my father to store so he could feed the villagers in times of poor crops. Nor was it the barge that brought jars of oil or bolts of linen for the Temple storerooms.

This boat seemed to have risen straight from the depths of the river, like a strange, exotic water lily, unfurling as the warmth of the sun touched its bud. Sunlight on its gold embellishments dazzled the eye. Every part of its wooden hull was carved and covered with patterns in bright carnelian, turquoise and brilliant blue. It slid forward as if propelled by some inner force, glistening and glinting in the early river mist like an apparition.

It was Ra's golden boat, come straight from the Underworld.

Then I heard the beat of oars against the water. And against the sun I saw the outline of men and the sprays of water-beads being flung like jewels from their paddles. It was a real boat with real oarsmen and a huge dark red sail embellished with the Double Crown of Egypt. As it came closer I saw the Eye of Horus decorating its bow and the name, *Dazzling Aten*, written in hieratic script along its side.

Queen Tiy's barge.

I held my breath, expecting to catch sight of her on the golden throne under the red canopy with the wings of her vulture crown sweeping the air. Why was she on the river so early? But as the barge came closer, I saw a man was sitting there. By his elaborate dress and crown and spangled leopard skin, I knew he was the Highest of High Priests, Wosret – the Most Powerful One.

The barge came straight towards the Temple jetty,

now lined with squabbling village boys reaching out to catch the ropes. In the prow stood the captain, bare-chested, wearing only a short linen wrap. A gingery beard jutted from his face like a tangled bush and met with a nest of hairy growth on his chest. He wore no wig and his equally matted red hair fell to his shoulders like a wild cloak and was tied at his forehead with a white band.

Then I noticed the men were *all* wearing the same headbands. The white headband of mourning.

Who had died? I whispered a quick prayer to Hathor – not only Goddess of the Moon, but also Goddess who carries the souls of the dead to the West.

Servants stepped off the boat and beat cymbals to ward off evil spirits ahead of the Highest of High Priests as he was carried ashore in a golden sedan chair, encrusted with lapis lazuli and turquoise and jewels of rainbow hue. The sand in his pathway was swept with a date-palm leaf and sprinkled with precious oils as he was set down.

My father came rushing down the path, already dressed in his Temple clothes, a broad gold band around his neck and the gold crocodile bracelets clasping his upper arms. I was pleased I had pleated

the linen of his tunic properly and left it under a heavy
board to flatten overnight.

He rushed forward and bowed. 'My Lord, Wosret.
Most Powerful One!'

The Highest of High Priests held up his hand and
the crowd fell silent. His high cheekbones and strong
nose with flaring nostrils gave his face the appearance
of carved wood rather than flesh. And his eyes under
the dark-lined eyebrows looked as if they had been
replaced with glass. Black obsidian set in a statue's
face. Lifeless, lizard eyes.

'Henuka. As Her Majesty, Queen Tiy's, trusted
Priest and Embalmer at the Temple of Sobek, I've
come to fetch you for a special embalming.'

My father bowed. 'It must be someone of great
importance for you to have come personally, my
Lord.'

Wosret's eyes gave nothing away. 'This I cannot
announce.'

'My daughter Isikara is my helper. If the embalming
is of great importance I'll need her assistance.'

Wosret's eyes flicked coldly in my direction but
moved quickly away again. Despite the sun on my
back, I felt a small shiver run through me.

'Then let her hurry. The weather is warm. We

mustn't delay. The bodies will not last.' He snapped his fingers at his servants and they stooped to lift his chair onto their shoulders once again.

'Bodies . . .?' I wanted to ask more, but my father's look silenced me.

'Kara, collect my instruments and resins of myrrh, hekenu and nesmen, bark of cinnamon and the cloves and oils that will be needed. And bring the Book of Temple Inscriptions. Then tie and seal the chest with clay so no one will meddle with it. And pack the ceremonial wig box and my pleated linen garments. Be ready to leave immediately.'

I squinted back at him. 'What about the crocodiles? The first moon appeared this morning before sunrise. It's the day of Ritual and offering to Sobek.'

My father shook his head. 'That must wait. The Highest of High Priests' demands come first. We must attend the embalming and ensure whoever has died has a safe passage to the Underworld.'

'Can it be Queen Tiy?'

'Sssh! Kara! Hold your tongue!'

I slid a quick look at the barge with its gleaming embellishments. 'But it's her boat.'

'What of it?'

'Why is *he* using her boat?'

'Tckk! You ask too many questions! Fetch my things. Be prepared to leave immediately. But change into a clean tunic first and wash the mud from your feet.'

I tossed my head. 'I can't help the mud! I've been checking the crocodile pool.'

He sighed deeply. 'How I wish your mother were here to show you how to behave! Tidy yourself now, collect my implements and remember – only speak when you're spoken to. Be quiet otherwise. Stand up straight. Keep your head bowed. Don't shrug your shoulders or toss your head if you don't agree with what's said. The Highest of High Priests, Wosret, is truly the Most Powerful One. Don't be impulsive and say the first thing that comes into your head! Bite back your tongue!'

These words still draw a bitter sigh from me now as I write them. If only I hadn't spoken so unwisely. If only I had heeded what he said!

CHAPTER THREE

ANUBIS ... JACKAL OF THE UNDERWORLD

The smell in the small antechamber next to the embalming chamber was vile – sickly sweet with undertones of rotting. Even the juniper oil burning in a chafing dish and the cone of perfumed wax that I had placed on my head could not mask it. It was a smell I knew well. A stench of rotting entrails, gut and stomach gases.

The room was small and hot. Even with my head completely shaved for the embalming ritual, sweat still prickled against my skin. I felt my stomach heave and fought the urge to vomit by tying a mask of linen tightly over my nose and mouth. Then I leaned over the chafing dish until the strong tang of juniper smoke caught in my throat.

Next to me, slimy lumps of bloodied organs lay in bowls, ready to be washed with palm oil and immersed in special herb solutions. But before I could prepare them for washing, the priests had to say the ritual incantations.

Whose organs were they?

They were all there, except for the heart. The heart was left in the body, being the seat of wisdom. I knew the secret incantations. What was taking place in the wabet chamber next door was supposed to be secret. But I knew that powerful spells would be read to implore the heart not to be separated from the body in the Afterlife.

The carved canopic jars were standing waiting to receive the other organs – the four sons of Horus. In the dimness of the antechamber, their eyes glowed like hungry creatures waiting to be fed. Hapi the Baboon with his yellow amber eyes would guard the lungs. Duamutef, the Jackal with red carnelian eyes, would guard the stomach. Qebehsenue, the Falcon with green verdite eyes, would guard the intestines and Imseti, the Man with blue lapis lazuli eyes, would guard the liver.

On the stone ledge were my father's instruments, still bloody from their work. The hook he had inserted through the nose to dislodge the brain tissue. The flint knife he had used to slice open the abdomen. The wooden adze he had employed to scrape out the lungs, stomach, intestines and liver from the inner cavity. He would have cleansed the cavity with palm wine, and then stuffed it with bruised myrrh, cassia, pounded cloves and salt to dry it out.

I'd watched his expert hands preparing the body of a crocodile for mummification. But this was different. For him to have been fetched by the Highest of High Priests, it must have been someone *very* important.

I pressed my clammy cheek up against the cold stone wall and waited. Just then I noticed a crack in the wall. A gap. I could see into the wabet chamber next door. I pressed my eye closer. The body of a woman lay on the stone embalming slab, surrounded by shaven-headed priests in linen tunics.

The slab was carved in the shape of a lion and sloped in such a way that the woman's feet were higher than the rest of her body. She lay with her slender neck hanging over the edge, completely naked, her limbs long and graceful even without the adornments of fine linen and jewellery. She seemed like a sleeping

31

princess, who might wake and bid her guardians out of her way. Yet the bloody incision glowing like a red garnet necklace across her lower stomach showed she was truly dead.

My mouth went dry. This was no ordinary person. Not with that red flaming hair!

They had shaved part of her scalp. To one side, all that beautiful hennaed hair had gone. On the other, it hung in a cascade of brilliant auburn that almost swept the floor – thick and wavy and textured, as if it had seen hours and hours of brushing with oils.

Beneath the woman's tilted head was a stone basin. The last liquid content of her brain dripped slowly into the basin from a hole made at the base of her skull. Her earlobes each had two holes. The double piercing of royalty. There was a ridge on her forehead as if something had rested there and left its own mark. The mark of a royal diadem? Yes . . . on her blazing head she'd worn the Royal Vulture Crown and the golden discs of the Sun-God Amun. In her hands she had held the royal sceptre.

There was no mistaking it. This was Queen Tiy! The most beautiful queen to ever rule Egypt. The most exalted woman in Egypt.

She was so beautiful it was said any man looking at

32

her simply fell in love, without her uttering a word. I'd seen her float past on her barge, wearing robes as translucent as a dragonfly's wings, thinner than finest gossamer, embellished with dazzling gold sequins, her narrow waist accentuated with broad, beaded belts, her long neck hung with necklaces of multiple rows of shimmering beads and gold amulets, sunlight catching stones of every hue on bracelets and armbands and rings. Two tall, white ostrich plumes set with gold sun discs standing upright on her head, making her taller than anyone around her, with the extended wings of her Vulture Crown sweeping back from her face.

Now I was standing closer to her than I could have ever dreamed. Seeing something not meant for my eyes. I was seeing her through the peephole, stripped of all her finery. Just the body of a woman in death.

I listened to the incantations and prayers as the priests walked around the body, sprinkling it with white powder. In the heat, putrefaction would be quick. The white natron salt would speed up the process of drying, so the flesh would not rot.

I knew the days of the rituals. The body would lie for forty days in the salt until all moisture was drawn from it. Afterwards it would be anointed with resin and juniper oil and beeswax. Then it would be wrapped in linen with the heart amulet and other precious amulets placed between the bindings. Finally there would be the Opening of the Mouth ceremony. Queen Tiy's mouth and eyes would be ritually reopened with the ceremonial adze, so her spirit could re-enter her body and breathe life back into it for her journey into the Afterlife.

The entire ritual took seventy days – the period between death and life, based on the length of time Sophet, the Dog Star, vanishes from the night sky. Sophet, the brightest of all stars, lurks below the horizon for seventy nights then finally creeps back into the sky just as the Great River begins to swell and bring down its life-giving black earth. The re-appearance of the star's light is a sign of rebirth and celebration.

After the Opening of the Mouth ceremony, Queen Tiy, reborn like Sophet, would continue her journey into the Underworld.

But now in the gloom of the wabet chamber, my eye picked up a group of figures standing like a pack of sinister jackals on upright legs. Each wore a terracotta mask with high-pointed ears, fierce-painted eyes and the sharp snout of Anubis. They stood nodding their heads and bowing awkwardly as they tried to see out of tiny holes cut into the terracotta below their snouts.

Suddenly I noticed a dark shape lying on another slab. I pressed my eye closer to the peephole.

It was a boy. A princely, leopard-skin cloak covered one shoulder and a jewelled broad-collar rested across his chest. In the strange greenish light his face seemed bruised and pale but handsome, with a strong profile, chiselled cheekbones and a beautifully formed mouth. There was no bowl beneath his head so I knew the embalming process hadn't begun.

An Anubis-headed priest bent over and put an ear to the boy's chest. As he glanced up, the painted eyes seemed to stare directly at me. I jumped back from the wall and held my breath. Then, with my heart pounding, I pressed my ear against the peephole instead.

A muffled voice reached me. 'His heartbeat is weak. But he still lives.'

It was my father's voice! I knew I couldn't risk him seeing the glint of my eye at the peephole, but still I could not stop myself from peering through. Yes . . . I recognised the gold crocodile bracelets on his upper arms. It was definitely my father.

Another jackal-headed priest nodded slowly. By the leopard-skin cloak he wore, I knew he was the Highest of the High Priests, Wosret, who had fetched us in the Royal Barge. 'The poison wasn't strong enough!' His voice rasped with annoyance.

Poison . . .? I listened hard.

'We'll have to help him to the Underworld with a small puncture directly into the heart. Nothing more than the thinnest of needles, of course.'

'We can't do that!' My father sounded agitated.

'Why not?'

'How will we be judged when we enter the Hall of Truths and Anubis holds the scales for us? Our own hearts will measure heavily against the ostrich feather of Maat. Our hearts will be tossed to Ammut and our souls damned for ever. Puncturing the heart is an act of murder.'

Murder . . .? My heart jumped up to my throat. My father, a murderer? I swallowed hard and pressed my eye to the spyhole again.

'Is giving poison not an act of murder?'

'Poison is not as violent as piercing the heart.'

'My dear Henuka, you split hairs.'

My father looked down at the boy on the slab. 'I can't allow his heart to be punctured.'

The Anubis figures – all except my father – clustered together. Their heads were clumsy and obviously heavy and difficult to carry. Every movement they made was slower than normal. They were whispering and nodding to each other.

The Highest of High Priests turned from the group of jackals. He held his head high so that he could look directly at my father through the tiny peepholes. 'We've conferred. We can't be judged for doing something that is right for the Kingdom. We can't allow him to live. He's weak. Egypt has no place for a weak King. His brother, Amenhotep, *must* be King. We can't allow rivalry between the brothers. Now that Queen Tiy is dead, this is the moment for Tuthmosis to die as well.'

Tuthmosis! My hands flew to my throat. The boy was the Royal Crown Prince! I held my breath and felt my heart pounding. What would my father answer?

'Tuthmosis is *not* weak. He walks with a limp, through no fault of his own. It was an accident. You know that!'

Wosret stood with his jackal-head thrown back. He appeared to be looking down his snout at my father. 'A limp is a sign of weakness. No country wants a disfigured Pharaoh. His death is right for Egypt. We do this for the love of his brother, Amenhotep, the Boy King.'

My father shook his head slowly and deliberately. 'Amenhotep is as young as the moon. He can't be King. On this slab we have the rightful heir. The *real* King.'

Wosret flourished his hand. I half expected to see leopard claws showing at the tips of his fingers. 'Amenhotep was named after his father. He was already the favoured son before his father died. Yes, he is young. But it's not Amenhotep who will rule – it's *us* . . . now that Queen Tiy is dead. She meddled too often in the affairs of the Temple of Karnak.'

My father bowed. 'She was Royal Wife to King Amenhotep the Third.'

Wosret flicked his hand. 'Yes, yes . . . but she was not easily swayed and since her husband's death she appointed too many of her family to the Temple. Even her brother was made Second Prophet at Karnak. Amenhotep, the new young King, will rule under our guidance. But in truth, *we* will be the real rulers of Egypt.'

The group of whispering jackals standing behind Wosret nodded in agreement.

'Thebes is a viper's nest. The Kingdom needs a new philosophy.'

'A new philosophy? What do you mean?' My father's voice sounded strained. Almost fearful.

Wosret shook his jackal-head like a dog trying to get rid of an annoying fly. 'I am the Highest of High Priests. It's up to me to change the course of history without *any* interference.'

'You presume too much.' There was a defiant tone to my father's voice.

'That's *your* belief. My fellow High Priests don't agree.'

There was an intense silence. Despite the heat I felt shivery.

'By your silence, I take it you know the other priests support me?'

'Surely—'

Wosret lowered his head. I seemed to hear an animal growl come from his throat as he interrupted. 'We can't have dissension. This is the *only* way!'

'What do you imply?' My father's voice was sharp now.

'If you disagree with Tuthmosis's death, for the love of Egypt you'll have to drink the Cup,' Wosret snapped.

'The Cup!' I heard my father's startled intake of breath.

I was too scared even to blink now. I felt the tension as everyone waited for Wosret to speak.

He looked directly at my father and nodded, his jackal ears tipping up and down. 'It's your duty to drink the Cup. Your soul will travel through the Underworld in peace then.' He spoke in a deep, flat voice, with a dismissive wave of his hand, as if this was merely an annoying procedure to be endured.

The Underworld? Suddenly I understood. My father was to be forced to drink *poison*! They were going to *kill* him. My mouth went dry. My knees turned as wobbly as the time I'd climbed too high in the mimosa tree. My head felt light and strange as I clutched onto the stone shelf against the wall.

Wosret spoke firmly, as if explaining something to an unruly jackal pup. 'Anubis will weigh your heart against Maat's ostrich feather and find your heart light with your good deed. Thoth, the Scribe of Truth and Wisdom, will record you as a man of honour. A man to be trusted. A man who has died for his country.'

I stuffed my fist into my mouth to prevent myself from crying out. *No! He's not to die! He's truthful and honest. My father needs no judging.*

In the lamplight I could see sweat gleaming on my father's bare shoulders. He bowed his jackal-head so that his snout almost reached his chest. 'I have no wish to die yet.'

'Ah yes . . .' Wosret spoke as if he was about to sip the finest gazelle-blood wine and was holding the glass thoughtfully up to the light before making a judgement. 'But *I* am the Highest of the High Priests. Let *me* be the judge of when you should die for the good of your country. You've done your work well as High Priest of Sobek's Temple. We'll be sorry to lose you.'

Lose him? They weren't *losing* him. They were *killing* him!

'Then why?' My father's voice cut abruptly through the silence.

Wosret shrugged. 'You're not in agreement with us. So I'm giving you the opportunity of dying an honourable death.'

Now the silence was broken only by the quiet drip of liquid falling from the back of the Queen's skull into the bowl below.

'Come on, Henuka! Be reasonable! Your journey will be pleasant. You'll accompany the great Queen Tiy, as well as her son, Tuthmosis. I can arrange for your burial chamber to be near theirs, adjacent to King Amenhotep's chamber. It's an *honour* to be chosen. Don't make me use force. Remember I am the Most Powerful One!'

My father bowed again. 'That does not escape me! But as a priest so long in service of the Great King, and his wife, Queen Tiy, I would deem it more of an honour to be able to continue with the embalming of Queen Tiy. Afterwards, if it's your wish, I'll offer myself to the Divine Crocodile, Sobek, at the Temple where I've served.'

I shuddered. What? Was I, as keeper of the sacred crocodiles, to be made to lead my father into the crocodile pit and watch them devour him? Impossible! I was numb with fright. The thought made me so light-headed I was definitely going to faint.

I clutched the wall for support.

Wosret answered smoothly. 'To die for Sobek won't suit. It'll take too long.'

My father glanced at him. 'In my experience, death by a crocodile is quick and fatal. It is *never* long!'

'It is not the *method* of death I object to, but the *time* it'll take to arrange for your return to the Temple of Sobek. Don't you see – the less that is known of your dissension, the more honourable your death will appear? We'll announce you were overcome by grief at the death of the Queen.'

Silence. I felt they might hear the thumping of my heart.

'Will you grant me one favour?'

Wosret sighed. 'We're wasting precious time discussing this, Henuka, when we should be getting on with it. Well – what is it?'

'Allow me to complete the embalming of Queen Tiy. It should not be entrusted to a lesser embalmer.'

For a moment Wosret seemed to hesitate. He made a delicate vault of his hands, with each finger-tip touching the opposite one in a mock gesture of thoughtfulness, knowing his silence held complete power in the chamber. Knowing too that my father was right, he bowed his head and sighed as if with great generosity. 'Very well. The favour is granted. But you are not to leave the wabet chamber until the embalming process is complete. The other High Priests will fetch the necessary liquids and ointments and oils from the Temple. And then, when the ritual is finished, *and* you have disposed of the boy, well . . .'

My father knelt and touched his jackal-head three times to the floor so that I heard the hollow sound of the terracotta ears knocking against the stone. 'So be it.'

What? *So be it?* Was he agreeing? Why didn't he fight

for his life? No! This could *never* take place! I pulled away from the spyhole and flung myself back against the wall. In my panic I swept a bowl off the shelf. As it fell to the stone floor, the terracotta shattered and Queen Tiy's entrails spilled out at my feet.

There was a moment of complete silence. I held my breath. Then a voice hissed, 'What was that?'

Suddenly the door from the wabet chamber was flung open. Two priests rushed in and grabbed me by the shoulders and pushed me forward into the presence of the jackal-headed men. 'She was spying. The Queen's entrails have been defiled.'

I couldn't see my father's eyes through the peepholes under the snout of his mask, but I felt his look. I shook off the hands of the priests. My eyes fixed on the Highest of High Priests. 'I heard everything! I know your plot!' I spat out. 'You're asking my father to be a *murderer*. And because he won't agree you want to kill him as well.'

'Isikara . . . keep silent! I beg you.'

Wosret turned to my father. 'A feisty girl, this daughter of yours.'

He walked slowly around me, looking me up and down with his dreadful jackal face. I clenched my jaw and stood up straighter with my arms at my sides, defying him to try and scare me with his jackal eyes and sharp jackal grin. I wouldn't flinch.

'Yes . . . a fine girl. Well-boned and strong, I see. It seems a waste to make her drink the poison cup as well.' He nodded his head towards my father as if in politeness. 'Not so, Henuka?'

My father kept silent. I could feel him willing me to be silent as well.

'You do not scare me, sir!' I spat the words at him.

'Ah, polite too!' he bowed his jackal-head at me. 'I'm charmed to be acquainted.' And then added, 'Even at this very sad time.'

I felt his hand run over the small of my back and down my thigh. The soft, unnerving touch of a leopard with its claws sheathed. I shrunk back from him. I wanted to hit out . . . spit in his face . . . clutch at his throat!

'It seems a waste for someone so polite and pretty to die so young . . . not so, Henuka?'

My father made no reply.

'But there are other options. She'd make a comely mistress.' Through the peep holes I caught the glint of his black obsidian snake-eyes as he grabbed my arms and pulled them behind me. 'Wouldn't you?'

I tried to twist free.

45

'Not just a comely mistress, but a fighter too, I see. Someone with spirit.'

I wanted to bite the hands that held me but I could not reach them. Instead I spat.

He spun me around to face him and raised his hand in the air as if to slap me, but then stopped. His jackal face was expressionless but his words were full of venom. 'You've defiled the floor of the *wabet*! Holy ground, already ritually washed. Ground that we brush our footsteps from, when we leave. Defiled by a slip of a girl!'

'She's young and thoughtless.' I hated to hear the note of begging in my father's voice.

Wosret stared at me from beneath his jackal snout. 'On second thoughts, Henuka, perhaps a life of luxury as my mistress is too kind for her. Perhaps she's better suited to being a slave. Slavery might pacify her spirit.'

A shiver ran down my back. He spoke of me in the third person – as if I was already an object to do with as he wished.

I narrowed my eyes. There was no stopping me now. 'I'll be no one's slave. Least of all *yours*! And never your mistress! I would rather kill myself first.'

'*That*, you may have to do,' his voice rasped back at me.

CHAPTER FOUR

THE OPENING OF THE MOUTH

The sound of footsteps echoed down the stone passageway as the priests left the wabet chamber. Then a clang of metal shuddered through the walls as the door that led to the Temple was bolted shut.

I spun around to face my father. 'You knew, didn't you? You knew about the poison.'

My father thrust off the terracotta mask. In the gloom his face was pale and pinched. He lifted his finger to his lips then went through the doorway into the antechamber and glanced around quickly to make sure no one had remained hidden.

He turned swiftly. 'Kara . . . Kara – what have you done? Listen carefully! They've gone back to the

Temple, but only for the ritual of collecting oils. They'll return soon. We haven't much time. Quick! You must do *exactly* what I tell you. There's no time for arguing. You must escape.'

'How, if they've locked the door?'

My father put his hands on my shoulders and gripped me firmly. 'I said *listen*! There's a secret doorway to a passage. It'll lead you out of here. It's your only chance. But you must take the boy with you.'

'The boy? Tuthmosis?'

My father nodded. 'He's not truly poisoned. As soon as I suspected the murder plot, I prepared another mixture for him to drink – one that merely put him into a deep sleep. I planned to fool the High Priests. I shouldn't have challenged Wosret, yet I *had* to prevent him from puncturing Tuthmosis's heart. The needle would truly have killed him. I was forced to speak out.'

'But—'

'Listen,' he whispered urgently, 'outside in the secret passage is the body of a poor peasant boy who died of natural causes last night. His mother was happy to be paid in exchange for having her son properly embalmed. I arranged this secretly with the help of a few other priests who discovered Wosret's plot and support my view. The boy's body will replace Tuthmosis's. The High Priests will think it him lying there. But instead, Tuthmosis will escape and later avenge his position and reclaim the throne.'

'But the priests will surely notice it isn't him.'

'Not immediately, in the dim light. The boy's eyes will be closed. He'll be dressed in the leopard cloak. But there's no time to waste. Now you're involved, the plan is even more urgent.'

'I'm sorry—'

My father waved his hand to silence me. 'You must escape, Kara! To be a slave to Wosret doesn't bear thinking about.'

The walls of the wabet chamber seemed to be closing in on me. I was feeling dizzy trying to keep up with what he was saying. 'I can't leave without you.'

'I'll follow. But first, I must arrange the body on the slab. It'll give you more time to get away. A chance of escape.'

'You keep talking about *me*. What about *you*?'

'I'll follow as quickly as I can.'

I shook my head. 'I can't go without you. Let me help with the body. We'll go together!'

'No!' he hissed. 'It's too dangerous. You must leave immediately.'

'But how will *you* get away?'

'Don't worry about me.' He gripped my shoulders and pulled me tight against his chest and then released me just as quickly. 'Here . . . take this.' He removed something from the girdle bag at his waist. 'My Senet gaming board. Be mindful of its messages. Now quick! Help me move Tuthmosis. I need his leopard cloak and his broad-collar.'

I wanted to stay clutching onto him but he pushed me away and began pulling Tuthmosis upright. 'Hurry! Get hold of him now.' He ripped the cloak from his shoulders and unclipped the broad-collar with its filigree of jewels and gold. 'Put your arm about his waist. Arrange his arm over your shoulder for support.'

The weight made me stagger. He was taller than I'd thought. I leaned up against the wall to steady myself. There was no time to give my father another glance. He went ahead of me and slid away a stone opening into a shadowy space lit by a small terracotta lamp.

Through the dimness I saw a dark lump at the bottom of the stairs. I turned my eyes away so as not to see the face of the peasant boy and concentrated on dragging Tuthmosis down the steps. By the time I steadied him against a wall at the bottom, my father had already scooped up the other boy. He couldn't bid me a proper farewell. Nor could I reach out to him. We were both weighed down by our burdens.

He nodded into the distance. 'At the fork, don't take the passage to the right. It leads to the workers' village. Go left. Take the lamp with you. Hurry! Your life depends on it!'

'What about . . .?' But he was already gone. I heard the sound of stone on stone as he rolled the secret door firmly behind him. The sound rang through the dark spaces ahead. I felt its vibration shudder through the stone floor beneath my sandals.

I was alone with Tuthmosis leaning heavily on my shoulders. The air was hot and heavy with a strange putrid smell and the ground mushy and slippery underfoot. Small scratching noises made me jump. Dark shapes scampered down the passageway ahead. Eyes caught and reflected in the flickering lamplight like red rubies.

Rats! The whole passage was full of them. I kicked at a dark shape that skimmed against my sandal. Suddenly something flew up at me out of the darkness. I ducked as it brushed my cheek and skimmed over my head with a high-pitched squeak. A bat!

I grasped the lamp and held it high with my free

hand. Clusters of them hung upside down from the ceiling vault like empty girdle pouches. Too many to count. I was grateful I wasn't wearing a wig, that my head was freshly shaven for the embalming rituals. The thought of the hooks on a bat's wing snaring me made me shudder.

'Tuthmosis, I can't do this alone. *Wake up!*' My voice echoed into the space. I shook him urgently. He remained like a stone against my shoulder. I began half dragging, half pushing him. His legs buckled and splayed in all directions. Then he started to shuffle along like a sleep walker. The passage was slippery with droppings. Hardly daring to breathe, I dragged him beneath the silent black pouches and prayed he wouldn't suddenly shout out and rouse them.

Rats scampered ahead of me, the skittering sound of their nails scraping stone and their menacing, long-tailed shadows dancing around the walls of the narrow passage in the lamplight.

I could hardly breathe. The space seemed to be getting smaller and smaller. The walls and ceiling closing in on me. Pressing the air out of my lungs. Pressing from all sides. Suffocating me.

I stumbled down some stone steps and propped Tuthmosis against a wall so I could catch my breath.

I listened for footsteps. But the silence was broken only by the squeak of rats.

Why had I spoken out so unwisely? What if my father didn't follow? What if I could never find my way out?

Tuthmosis began murmuring.

'Are you awake?' His head lolled against my shoulder as I tried to push him upright. 'I can't carry you any longer. Do you hear me? Wake up!' I shook him urgently, then without thinking, I slapped him. A sharp slap on both cheeks.

My hand jumped back in fright. Had I lost my senses? He was the Crown Prince – son of King Amenhotep and Queen Tiy of Egypt! I should have been bowing to him, yet here I was slapping him. I could be put to death for less than this!

I held up the lamp to see if I had left a mark. Both cheeks were red. His eyelids were fluttering. What if he knew? For a brief moment he opened his eyes, and then closed them again.

'No! I beg you! Please, *please*, wake up!' I held the lamp closer. Beneath the dark lashes and the rim of black kohl, his eyes were a strange shade of pale blue. I nudged him again. 'Tuthmosis, can you see anything? Your eyes seem odd. They're blue!'

53

He nodded with his lids half closed.

'Impossible! Egyptians don't have blue eyes.'

He rested his head against the wall again and sighed. His breathing became deep and even.

I shook him. 'Don't dare go back to sleep. We *have* to find a way out of here.'

He shivered and started to grumble about something. Then, without a look in my direction, he demanded, 'Are you one of the Palace slaves? It's cold here. Fetch my cloak.'

'I'm not a slave! Listen! Wosret tried to poison you.'

He shook his head like a dog trying to shake off water, then turned and looked at me as if he was emerging through a thick mist. 'What did you say?'

'Wosret tried to poison you.'

'Wosret?' His eyes opened wide. 'Wosret is the Highest of High Priests? Don't be ridiculous! It can't be true. He's my royal mentor.'

'Do you remember anything?'

He frowned. 'At my mother's deathbed, Wosret offered me a chalice to drink for comfort.'

'*Comfort?* He made you drink *poison*. Listen . . .' I told him as quickly as I could about my father replacing the poison with another mixture and replacing him with the dead boy's body.

He shook his head again. 'Impossible! It's ridiculous. You've made it up. Where are my servants? And who are you? Why should I believe you?'

'I don't care if you don't believe me! Stay here then! I can't waste any more time. I'll find my own way out. If it wasn't for my father, I wouldn't be bothered with you at all!'

My outburst roused him from his stupor. He lifted his head sharply and glared back at me, then gave an abrupt shrug of his shoulders. 'I could have you put to death for treason for such words.'

'*Treason?* I'm trying to help! You don't seem to understand the danger!'

His icy look made me realise I had spoken too freely. I bowed my head and went on hurriedly. 'I implore you . . . they'll be coming after us soon!'

'Do you speak the truth?'

'By the white feather of Maat, every word is true. You *must* believe me!' I glanced back quickly into the darkness. 'My father is supposed to follow. But he hasn't. We must escape. Our lives depend on it. But I can't see an exit. We're in a dead end.' I held the lamp higher. Rats scampered away from under my feet. As I swung it around, my heart jumped. Wosret loomed up through the flickering shadows in front of me. Then I swallowed hard as I realised it was only a painting of Anubis. We were in a small vault.

'This *must* lead to a burial chamber.'

'How do you know?'

'Look at the paintings.' I pointed at the ceiling. 'There's Nut, Goddess of the Sky, lighting the darkness and Horus touching the mouth of a mummy with an adze. This is an antechamber before the journey to Ra. There *has* to be a hidden door. A mouth to the Afterlife.'

Tuthmosis seemed distracted. He pointed at the floor. 'Those turquoise tiles ... look at the way they're arranged. Three rows of ten. Like the thirty squares in a game of Senet.'

Suddenly I remembered my father's board. I reached into my girdle pouch and brought it out. 'My father said this would help me.'

The cedar-wood box was long and narrow with a turquoise and ivory inlay. On one side was a drawer. I slid it open. Inside were carved agate pieces. Tuthmosis picked up one and rubbed it between his fingers.

'What are you doing?'

'I'm trying to remember something. Senet is a game of passage. Your father must've given it to you for a reason.'

56

'A game of passage?'

He nodded. 'It follows a journey along the thirty squares. Some squares are more important than others. Look.'

I held the lamp above the box. Drawings were incised in the turquoise squares and the fine grooves were inlaid with ebony. Each drawing was precise and perfect. In one square was the ibis-headed Thoth. In the middle was a figure of a man in a boat with his head turned backwards. Near it were a frog and a scarab beetle and the symbol for a maze or a labyrinth. The third square from the end had wavy water marks. On the last square was an image of Ra.

'It makes no sense. It's only a game. We haven't time!'

'Games have a beginning and an end.'

'So?'

'The floor is a Senet board. Thirty tiles, in three rows of ten. We have to find the end square.'

'Why?'

'It's where you leave the board to meet Ra. It'll be marked with his image. If we find the end tile, we've found our escape.'

I wanted to stamp my feet with frustration. Instead, I kicked aside the dust and rat droppings and bent down to peer at the squares. 'Nothing. Not even the tiniest mark or pattern. You're wrong. This is a dead-end. We've missed a turning. We must retrace our steps.'

'No! Find the Ra square. There are only two possibilities for it. Facing either end, it'll be the bottom left square.'

Taking a deep breath and trying to stay calm and focused, I traced my fingers across the left tile on the end nearest to me and felt around its edges. 'Nothing, except rat droppings!' I rushed to the opposite end and held the lamp high. The turquoise colour of the left tile was worn. My eyes flew to the narrow, shadowed gap around the tile's edges. Then I caught Tuthmosis's look.

'You're right! This *has* to be it!'

CHAPTER FIVE

THE COBRA GODDESS

The tile was heavy. Eventually it loosened and I eased it aside. Below it, rough steps led into a dark, narrow space that sloped downwards and ended in a stone wall.

'What can you see?' Tuthmosis's left leg dragged as he struggled down the steps.

'Another dead-end. The passage is sealed.'

He traced his fingers over one of the stones. 'There's a pattern here. The lines are crosshatched. A symbol for a labyrinth perhaps?'

'It *has* to lead somewhere!' I hammered at the stone. Then began to claw at its edges, searching for a place to loosen it with my nails. 'It's useless!' I held out my hands to Tuthmosis. My fingertips were raw and bleeding.

'We need something sharp to help gouge it out,' he said.

'Wait! There's this.' I drew out my mother's bronze mirror from my girdle pouch. At the last moment before leaving the Temple of Sobek, I'd snatched it up. The thought of having something my mother once held was comforting. The handle was in the shape of Hathor. The reflecting disc was the large moon held by the horns on her head, so when you looked into the mirror, Hathor's face showed below your own.

'You took a *mirror* to my mother's embalming?'

'I meant no disrespect. I had no time to think about whether or not it was correct to bring a mirror into the wabet chamber.'

Tuthmosis laughed. 'My mother would've been delighted. She spent hours in front of her mirror every day, watching her attendants arrange each strand of hair!' He pointed at the stone. 'Quick! Dig around the stone! Hurry!'

I jabbed at the edges of the stone with Hathor's feet and sent her a silent prayer to ask for help in holding my tongue. Tuthmosis had the manner of someone used to giving orders and the carelessness of someone used to having them obeyed. He was treating me as his servant. I wasn't sure how long I would be able to remain silent.

My hands were scraped raw by the time the stone eventually loosened. I wiped them against my tunic and rubbed the mirror clean.

Tuthmosis looked at it and shrugged. 'A few scratches perhaps. The mirror might not be quite as perfect as before . . . but the face that looks into it will still be perfect.' He smiled fleetingly at me before pushing against the stone with his shoulder. 'Here . . . help me! It's heavy.'

I bit my tongue. No thought to ask my name but already giving orders and passing comments on my face.

We eventually managed to shift the stone. Tuthmosis held up the lamp and peered through the narrow gap in complete silence. His back muscles gleamed with sweat and dust.

'What do you see?'

'My father's tomb.'

'It can't be!'

He turned to face me. 'It is! I played here while it was being built. It took more than ten years. I came whenever he made an inspection with his Chief Vizier.

I watched the vaults being carved into the mountain, the walls being smoothed, the sculptors at work, the artists as they painted and the scribes writing holy spells on the walls. It's *his* tomb!'

I squinted through the shadowy lamplight at him. 'How can you be so sure? It could be any king's tomb.'

He gave me a look. 'Do you think I don't know the exact details of my own father's tomb? His sarcophagus is carved of red granite.'

'A sarcophagus is always carved of dark stone – *never* red.' I pushed past him and began squeezing myself through the narrow opening.

He grabbed hold of my tunic. 'Stop! Don't dare enter.'

'Why not?'

'You'll destroy the tomb's sanctity. How'll my father reach the Afterlife if we disturb him?'

I turned fiercely. 'We *have* to enter. It's our only escape.'

Tuthmosis's blue eyes stared back coldly. In the lamplight they reflected like moonstones. For a moment I felt afraid of their intensity. Then I tossed my head. 'You have to trust me.' I turned away. Then as an afterthought I threw back at him, 'And you might ask my name.' The words sounded silly after I'd spoken them.

'Well – what is it?'

'Isikara. And you should know that just because you're the son of a king doesn't make me your servant!'

Our eyes stayed locked. Then he spoke my name as if tasting the sound of it. 'Isikara . . . we both have to trust each other.' Without another word, he pushed in front of me.

I followed him through the opening, edging my way along in the darkness, keeping one hand on the wall, feeling the stone sharp under my fingertips.

There in the lamplight, stood the silent sarcophagus.

My breath caught. It was as red as oxblood. Red granite indeed!

I shuddered, thinking of what lay beneath. The golden mummy case, within it another golden case, and another and another until, in the final one, the mummy of King Amenhotep. Wrapped in the finest of linens, decked with jewels, his arms across his chest holding the gold staff and crook of a pharaoh, his face covered with a golden mask and on his forehead the cobra rearing up, ready to strike.

We were in the heart of the burial chamber – deep below the mountains of Thebes.

We stood in our tiny pool of light. Beyond its edges the darkness stretched upwards to a ceiling painted dark blue and scattered with stars. Around us, other vast empty spaces disappeared into thick blackness. The sheer magnitude of it choked all sound from my throat.

Tuthmosis turned abruptly. His footsteps echoed against some stone steps that led between two huge square pillars into an area with yet more pillars. I jumped back as King Amenhotep loomed in front of us, staring straight into my eyes. He wore a magnificent girdle, set with real lapis lazuli and turquoise. A shining gold and obsidian pectoral plate hung against his chest.

On his brow was the striking cobra – the Cobra Goddess. Her red, ruby eyes held me in her power. Above was inscribed . . .

Beware the Cobra Goddess who guards
the Royal King and His treasures.
The Cobra Goddess anoints Your head, O
Pharaoh, with her flames. She rises up on the left
side of Your head and she shines from the right

*side of Your Temple each and every hour of the
day. Through her, the terror which You inspire
is increased. She will never leave You.*

I stood transfixed. As I stared into those fiery eyes,
I felt I was invoking her anger. Standing waiting for
her deadly bite. I clasped my arms across my chest and
held my hands to my throat for protection.

Such was her power!

She sat on the Pharaoh's brow with her hood
flaring. Ready to spit poison at all his enemies. Ready
to burn them with her fiery glare. But she was a fickle
goddess. Not just the defender of the Pharaoh. She
could be *against* him as well. Her bite could be
the deadly device used by Anubis to cause the
Pharaoh's death. No one would know – so great was
her danger.

Hathor was drawing Amenhotep along, wearing
an exquisite dress of turquoise beads which clung in
a cloudlike net to the curves of her body. She was
carrying the moon on her head, a turquoise broad-
collar encircled her neck and flaring cobras, with
burning carnelian eyes, dangled dangerously from
her ears.

My eye caught the glimmer and sparkle of things

heaped in two side-chambers leading off the vast vault.

Tuthmosis saw my glance. 'My father's treasure. His gold chariot for the ride across the heavens. His gold barque to carry him along the river of the Underworld. His throne embellished with ivory, bloodstones and lapis lazuli. His gilded cheetah bed. His gold hunting bow, along with a gold statue of his favourite hunting dog, embedded with emerald eyes.'

'So much?' My voice echoed into the dark cavernous spaces.

'Even more. Linen, leopard-skins, gold-bladed jewel-encrusted daggers, headrests of glass, chests filled with goblets, scarabs, amulets, necklaces, bracelets and breastplates, alabaster jars of wine and olive oil, caskets of ox and goose meat. All has been catered for.' Tuthmosis nodded towards some paintings. 'And the princes of Syria, Palestine, Babylon and Nubia lavished him with gifts of turquoise, amethysts, perfumed oils, gold, ivory and skins as well. But enough – we must hurry!'

We passed from a second antechamber into another passageway and were stopped from going further by a well-shaft in a sharp right turn. It was wide enough to prevent anyone jumping across it and its sides fell straight down into the heart of the mountain.

Deep below, I caught an oily black reflection of water. There were no footholds to give access to the opposite side.

'How'll we cross to the tomb entrance?'

'Stone slabs originally bridged the well. They were removed to protect my father's treasure. But there's another way. My father sculpted a series of vaults with sliding doors and secret passageways. These were meant only for his trusted Vizier, so he could enter and inspect the well and ensure it collected and prevented water from running down the passages into the burial chamber.'

'The builders must've known about it too.'

'Each team worked on a section of the labyrinth. No one but the Vizier knew the final plan.'

'No one but the Vizier and *you*!'

Tuthmosis ducked behind a small pillar. A statue of Anubis glared at us from a niche. A metal collar around Anubis's neck was linked by a heavy chain to a ring in the stone floor. Tuthmosis pushed against the niche and it swung open.

'A secret door?'

He nodded. 'When the door closes, the statue swings back to rest in its original place.'

As it was about to shut behind us, I thought of

something. 'Wait! What about my father? How'll he find it?'

Tuthmosis pulled off his sandals and wedged them in place in the doorway so that a small gap showed.

I was being too hopeful. I had lost track of time. It was hard to tell how long we had been in the labyrinth. Perhaps even more than a day. My father should have caught up with us by now. Perhaps the High Priests had returned and discovered his plot. I couldn't bear to think about it.

We stepped into a cavern of chambers with crypts and niches and winding passages leading in every direction into darkness. Our lamp had no way of casting light in such a vast space. Vaults and stairs and images of gods and statues receded into the gloom.

Nothing moved. Just a deathly silence and our footsteps against the stone.

I knew about labyrinths. Katep and I had secretly entered one but hadn't dared go beyond the first chamber. They were complicated spaces planned to protect burial chambers. Passageways wound backwards and forwards in bewildering patterns. Doorways showed the way ahead and at the same time tricked a thief to go back along the same passage.

'Which way?' I whispered.

Tuthmosis guided my hand across a stone wall. I felt three small indentations.

'I carved these at every point where a decision has to be made. This route goes all the way to the Great River so my father's *ka* can escape.'

Tuthmosis edged forward. It wasn't as easy as he made out. I sensed a moment of doubt each time he felt for the three marks. This wasn't the game he had played as a child, where he could call out and his father's Vizier would come for him. In the twists and turns of the labyrinth, we could be lost for ever.

I followed close behind him, my heart thumping in my ears. What if someone was coming towards us from the river?

Suddenly a terrifying rumble echoed through the passageways – as if the entire labyrinth was collapsing. I clutched Tuthmosis's arm as I tried to see into the darkness.

'We're trapped?'

He shook his head. 'It's a trick to scare thieves. It's only stones rolling around in a jar that falls from a pulley. I forgot about it. The pulley was triggered when we passed through the last doorway.'

We groped our way forward again.

When a scent of papyrus mixed with the smell of

sun-baked earth came wafting towards me, I knew at last we were near the end. A glimmer of light drew me. I stumbled ahead of Tuthmosis and began to run. We had finally made it.

Then I stopped short. A metal grid barred the end of the passageway. We really *were* trapped this time. I rushed forward, gripped the bars and shook as hard as I could.

'It's useless!' I bellowed over my shoulder. *Useless ... useless ...* I heard my voice echo back into the darkness as I crumpled against the ground. 'We're locked in!' I sobbed. *Locked in ... locked in ...* 'For ever!' *For ever ... for ever ...*

CHAPTER SIX

THE FESTIVAL OF SOPHET

Tuthmosis came up behind me.

'Shhh!' he hissed. 'Are you trying to get us caught? Someone will hear you!' He felt along a hidden ledge and brought out a key in the shape of an ankh. 'My father's Vizier told me about this.'

I spun around to face him. 'But you couldn't be *sure* it was there, could you? You took a risk! Curse you, Tuthmosis! Why didn't you warn me there would be a locked gate?' My voice was coming out in gasps. I wanted to shake him.

'I said we had to trust one another.' He fitted the key into a lock and turned. The grid swung open. 'Now listen! This leads into the grounds of the Palace near my father's Mortuary Temple. We can't remain in Thebes. It's too dangerous. We need a boat to travel upstream towards Nubia, beyond the borders of Egypt. We'll be going against the current but the wind blows upstream and will be in our favour.'

I shot a look at him. 'Nubia? That far?' Suddenly I was fearful. The passageway had been a link to my father. Listening for his footsteps, intent on our own escape, I hadn't given a thought to what we would do afterwards. Now, we were truly leaving my father behind. 'Do we have to go *that* far?'

Tuthmosis nodded. 'If what you say about Wosret is true, it's the only way to escape him and the High Priests.'

'You'll have to disguise yourself as a girl.'

'A girl? Never!'

'A boy with a limp and blue eyes is a giveaway. They'll know it's you. You'll need a girl's tunic and wig and we'll need a boat.'

'I know someone who'll help. She's not Egyptian. She came from Mitanni in the entourage of Taduk-hepa, daughter of the Prince of Naharin Satirna, who was sent to be my father's wife. We're friends. I trust her. Stay hidden here, while I find her.'

I shook my head. 'I'm coming with you.'

72

'It'll be quicker if I go alone. There are guards and guard dogs.'

'I'm not afraid.'

After the darkness of the labyrinth, it was like step-ping into a strange dream. The light seemed too bright, the air too perfumed with mimosa, and the drone of bees too heavy and loud. Below us was the Mortuary Temple, its gold walls and silver paving glinting in the sunlight. A phalanx of glistening black granite lionesses led to its silvered doors. These were guarded by two colossal stone statues of Amenhotep. Even from this distance they completely dwarfed the entrance.

With a quick sweeping glance, I took in the distant fields and the gardens laid out with date palms, the row upon row of green arbours heavy with grapes, orchards lush with apricots and pomegranates, fields of lilies – each bud staked so it wouldn't droop – roses in every hue from soft cream through to flaming orange and red, darker than blood.

Suddenly I realised what I was searching for.

The entire landscape lay silent. There were no people at the Mortuary Temple, nor any labourers working or hoeing or leading irrigation water.

I glanced towards the Great River and saw the reason. It was covered with sails wafting back and forth like hundreds of pale butterflies. On the opposite bank, a mass of people was moving along the sphinx-lined avenue that led from the river to the Temple of Karnak. On either side of its gateway, huge pennants of the Sun-God, Amun, fluttered from the massive cedar flag posts.

A sound of music, the shirring of sistrum rattles and the voices of women came floating up to us on the breeze.

I frowned at Tuthmosis, then suddenly remembered. 'Sophet! The Dog Star must've risen! It's the Festival of Sophet! Thebes is celebrating the rising of Sophet and the rising of the flood waters. Amun has to be thanked for saving the country from famine!'

'Then let's hurry! The Palace will be empty. Everyone will have joined the procession.'

Along the river I saw the red sails of the Royal Barge. I curled my fingers to my eyes to cut the glare and focused on the figures on deck, scanning them for any sign of my father.

'Do you think he's there?'

'Who?'

'My father.'

74

Tuthmosis shielded his eyes as well. 'It can't be! It is.' I saw him stiffen. 'My brother's on the boat! Curse him! He already wears *my* crown – the Royal Ceremonial Atef Crown. Look, its ostrich feathers are topped by gold Atum discs. It's normally kept for special ceremonies. All you said must be true. Wosret has lost no time!'

The sound of the sistrums came to us like reeds brushing in the breeze. But above the music, I heard another sound that sent a shiver through me. It was the eerie moan of the wind as it whistled between the stone cracks of the two giant statues of Amenhotep. The plaintive wail added its own voice to the celebration.

Even after death, Tuthmosis's father could still be heard!

We ran between tall papyrus reeds and gained the shadows along the walls of the garden. For the first time I saw how scarred Tuthmosis's left leg was, but the rest of his body was well-muscled and his limp didn't slow him down.

There was nobody about. Not even guard dogs. We came upon a menagerie of wild antelope and strange, tall, giraffe creatures. In separate enclosures, I caught glimpses of lions with huge dark manes. But there was no time to stop as Tuthmosis hurried me through an elaborate maze of linked cages. Around us the air rustled and rang with strange animal sounds and exotic squawks. Brilliant-feathered birds flashed against the foliage and monkeys jumped from branch to branch in fluted shafts of sunlight.

Tuthmosis gave a sharp whistle. The creatures fell silent and from behind a high stone wall came an answering call.

'Who is it?' I whispered.

'It's her. The girl.'

'Why isn't she at the procession?'

But Tuthmosis had already disappeared through a gate. I followed him into a courtyard filled with flowers and trees and paintings on the walls of still more flowers and trees. At my feet rills of water full of small fish trickled through paving stones painted with more fish. The courtyard seemed filled with every kind of tree, flower and creature. There was no way of knowing what was real, and what was painted.

But the girl was real. She was quite the most exotic creature I had ever laid eyes on.

Her linen robe was woven with dyed red threads and tasselled along the edge. Different to anything worn in Thebes. And her sandals, made from plaited papyrus, were drawn up sharply in the front in the shape of a boat's prow. I imagined them ploughing through the sands of some faraway desert. In her hand she held a broken sistrum handle in the image of Hathor. Metal discs from the sistrum lay scattered at her feet.

She turned pale at the sight of us. 'It can't be! They said you were dead!' She rushed forward and bowed low over Tuthmosis's feet so that the plaited strands of her wig swept into a rill and dragged wet marks across the paving.

He helped her up.

'It's truly you! I can't believe it. People are wearing white headbands of mourning for both you and Queen Tiy! Wosret has announced your death.'

'He lost no time!'

The girl nodded. 'The rooms of the Middle Palace are already prepared for your brother even though he still wears the sidelock of youth. He's been given a leopard-skin robe of office and wears the Royal Ceremonial Atef Crown. The girl Queen Tiy chose is living in the Palace. She'll be given the Sceptre of the Lily to carry in her left hand today at the ceremony.'

'Nefertiti?'

'They plan a royal wedding.'

'But Nefertiti was chosen for me!'

The girl nodded and went on quickly. 'Today your brother is to be presented to Amun at Karnak. He'll be named King Amenhotep. Everyone has joined the procession. I was late. My sistrum broke—'

'What? The priests are going to the innermost sanctuary of Amun, the Most Secret of Places, with *my brother?*'

I saw the flare of anger in Tuthmosis's eyes. I knew what this meant. The priests would lead his brother away from the eyes of the common people through the dazzling painted halls and mammoth columns reflected in the silvered floors, into the sanctuary of the Supreme God, Amun. A mysterious secret ritual would confirm the new Pharaoh's powers. Afterwards the statue of Amun would be carried by the priests to the Royal Barge and taken upstream to the Temple of Luxor. In the darkest recess of Luxor the new Pharaoh would meet his Royal *ka* – the spirit of his very inner being that we ordinary mortals only meet after death, when we go to be with the gods. But a king is privileged. In this secret place he meets his *ka* face to face and then emerges a God-King, blessed by Amun – the Sun-God's living image on earth. To be obeyed by everyone.

I couldn't help crying out, 'You *can't* allow this to happen!'

His eyes were as cold and flinty as river pebbles as he caught my look. 'I'll fight to win my Kingdom back – be sure of that.'

The girl shook her head. 'You can't! They're too powerful. The priests will *never* let you return. They've told everyone you're dead. They'll make sure you die so their plan remains in place.'

'I'll gather my own army against them.'

'An Egyptian army? Never. Everyone is too terrified.'

'There are armies beyond Egypt's borders, who will stand by me. If I can't enlist the support of Egypt, I'll enlist the support of Egypt's enemies. But I need your silence and your help *urgently*.'

'You have both!' Her eyes darted towards me.

He saw her look. 'Kara is coming with me. Are there servants about?'

She shook her head. 'None. They're all at the procession. The only guards left behind have raided the storehouse and are already in sodden stupors, quite drunk on Palace beer. They wouldn't know the difference between an ox and their grandfathers right now. Without your mother to keep order, everything is upside down. And with the news of your death as well, the Palace is in turmoil.'

'The dogs?'

'Chained up. The guards wanted to be free of bother.'

'Quick then, Ta-Miu! We'll go to my mother's quarters. We're least likely to be disturbed there. Isikara needs a wig. Nothing fancy. Something for protection against the sun, as well as a disguise. I need one too. One that makes me look like a peasant girl. And we need a boat.'

He turned abruptly and led the way through a massive doorway into a maze of interior rooms. The girl disappeared down a passageway and Tuthmosis drew me quickly on.

Ta-Miu? So that was her name.

CHAPTER SEVEN

TA-MIU ... THE GIRL FROM MITANNI

Each room seemed more vividly painted, more glistening with glazed tiles and brighter with inlays of painted plaster than the last. There was too much to take in with a single hurried glance.

I ran breathlessly on through passages lined with decorated boxes, each with a plate naming the papyrus inside. Many more than in my father's Temple library. My eyes swept over the hieratic script as I ran. *The Book of Dreams. The Book of the Black-maned Lion. The Book of Plagues.* They were all there. Too many for one man to ever read in a lifetime. I wanted to stop and look but Tuthmosis was already far ahead.

At the very heart of the Palace was an audience

room so vast I was scared to look up. The entire length of its ceiling was painted with the huge wings of the Vulture Goddess, Nekhbet, its vault supported by mammoth columns adorned with lotus flowers unfurling their great petals against the ceiling. Under our sandalled feet, portraits of Egypt's enemies flashed by – trodden on daily by the Pharaoh as he passed through this room to his canopied throne.

Beyond this were the royal bedchambers.

Queen Tiy's bedroom was painted a brilliant red. As we entered I was overpowered by the heady perfume of hundreds of white lilies filling urns everywhere. Hovering over us with giant outstretched wings was the Vulture Goddess again, painted on the ceiling in bright, vibrant colour. Crouched on the floor, snarling up at me with teeth and claws bared and terrifying eyes, was a lion. I stood paralysed until I realised it lay flat, without flesh or muscle.

I gasped as I saw Queen Tiy's feathered Vulture Crown right before me on a special stand. My fingers ached to touch it. To lift it up and feel the weight of it on my head and to sense the sweep of its wings, glittering with gold and jewels, at either side of my temple.

I glanced at Tuthmosis, wondering how he felt being

so close to his mother's things. But he held himself stiffly, as if passing through a stranger's chamber, and urged me quickly past.

There were cats curled up everywhere. Lying on the drapes that covered a huge, lion-clawed bed and sleeping on cushioned chairs. One rubbed itself against Tuthmosis's legs. I saw a faint smile cross his face. 'My mother loved cats. She shaved her eyebrows the day her favourite cat died. She had all her cats embalmed after death and buried in sacred receptacles.'

I slid a sideways glance at him. 'Do you have a favourite cat? You called the serving girl Ta-Miu – little kitten.'

He shrugged and bent down to stroke the cat purring at his ankles. 'It's just a pet name.'

Is the girl your favourite? I wanted to ask, but bit my lip. 'She's pretty . . .' is all I said.

My breath caught as we came to an inner sanctum. Everything any woman could desire lay waiting for the hands of the Queen – as if she might walk into the room at any moment.

Small chests, each intricately inlaid with ivory and mother-of-pearl, held cosmetic spoons, kohl tubes, eyebrow tweezers, curling clips, combs, delicate glass phials of perfume and turquoise-glazed offering bowls.

Ostrich fans and an array of amulets, bracelets, rings and jewelled broad-collar necklaces, curved like multicoloured rainbows, spilled out onto tables.

Without being able to stop myself, I dug my fingers into the jewels and brought out a ring with the largest amethyst I've ever seen. I picked up an ivory comb, expecting to feel the warmth of the Queen's hand still on it. A single strand of bright hennaed hair twirled through its teeth. I traced my fingers over a translucent alabaster cosmetic spoon in the form of a swimming girl propelling a gazelle-shaped container, and lifted the finely carved head that formed the lid. Its hollowed belly still held perfumed wax.

Just then the serving girl returned. She took the lid from my hands and replaced it, moving with the quick hover of an iridescent dragonfly.

The plaited side pieces of her wig swung against her cheeks like delicate beaded curtains. Her lips were touched with red ochre, and her dark mysterious eyes, rimmed with kohl, were made darker still by the brilliant colour she wore beneath her eyelids. It wasn't the usual green malachite eye-paste worn at important rituals to symbolise new life. Her eye-paint was bright turquoise. As brilliant as the flash of a kingfisher, making her eyes appear like dark reflecting pools.

She handed me a fresh tunic made of coarse, unbleached linen and offered a tray of some apricots and thin slices of duck that tasted smoky. Tuthmosis moved around the room restlessly.

'Aren't you going to eat? It's delicious.'

'There's no time!'

The girl slid open the catches on a box. 'I would've brought two of my own wigs but they're too distinctive. These are from the servants' quarters. They've already been powdered with cinnamon against lice and perfumed with rose oil.'

'Lice—?'

'We need sandals.' Tuthmosis interrupted. 'I've lost mine and Isikara's won't last the journey.'

'I've brought some.' She glanced at me. 'For you – two pairs of mine. Your feet are the same size.' The ones she held were normal, flat-woven ones, not the upturned kind she was wearing. She looked up at Tuthmosis. 'Two pairs of your own sandals as well.'

I eyed her. Who was this girl that she went about so freely in Tuthmosis's rooms and knew where to find his sandals?

'What about the boat? And food?' Tuthmosis asked.

'There's a reed boat waiting for you at the causeway

closest to the South Gate. The canal will take you directly south to join the Great River further upstream. With luck you won't come across anyone returning from Karnak or Luxor. There are throwsticks and harpoon spears in the boat to catch waterfowl and fish. I've put food in a basket as well and skins to keep you warm.' She glanced across at me. 'And a small casket of almond and cinnamon oil to protect you from the sun and wind.'

The girl had thought of everything.

She smiled at me, suddenly. 'Would you like kohl to protect your eyes from the glare and a little of my turquoise eye-paste?'

Tuthmosis clicked his tongue. 'There's no time for this! We must leave. They'll be returning soon.'

'Wait!' I touched the girl's arm. 'I must ask something. Have you news of my father, the Priest at the Temple of Sobek?'

She shook her head. But when I searched her face, her eyes seem to say something else. She shrugged. 'No one is sure of anything. One moment it's said we'll be sent back to Mitanni, the next it's whispered we'll all be made concubines to the new Pharaoh.'

I glanced at Tuthmosis to gauge his reaction to this news. His face was set hard and determined. He said nothing, but tugged at me. 'Come now, Isikara! We must hurry! Already there could be a search out for us.'

Suddenly I felt uneasy, and torn in two different directions. Maybe my father would still come. I glanced at Tuthmosis. 'Can't we wait? Just until tomorrow? The sun's already low. The river might not be safe at night.'

He shook his head. 'We can't risk being discovered. You heard Ta-Miu. They've already announced my death. They'll kill us if we're found.'

She nodded. 'He's right. The High Priests won't hesitate to get rid of you.'

Suddenly I felt fearful for her. 'And you? They might kill you for helping us.'

'I'll have to risk it.'

'Come with us!'

'No!' Tuthmosis glanced coldly at me. 'It'll be difficult enough to escape with just you – but I'm duty bound because of what your father did for me. Three of us would be impossible.'

So I was a burden! For a brief moment we stood eyeing each other.

Ta-Miu broke the tension. She reached up to Tuthmosis with her small, delicate hands. 'Go carefully!' she whispered. I saw her slip something to him from her girdle bag.

I turned away, not wanting to watch such a private moment. As I did, I noticed a small tattoo on her left shoulder. It was the outline of a cat. Yes . . . she was truly Ta-Miu. *His* Ta-Miu.

We went quickly down the pathway to the causeway, our footsteps slapping against the stone and echoing in the stillness as we ran.

A tall figure loomed up out of the shadows. 'Oi! Stop!'

I smelled fumes of palm wine on his breath – a guard so drunk, he could hardly stand. He came very close and peered into our faces with unfocused eyes. 'Where are you going?'

My heart stood still. Tuthmosis had not yet put on his disguise. He would be recognised. But before we could say anything, the man's legs gave way beneath him. He fell into a stupor at our feet and we skirted quickly past him.

We found the reed boat as Ta-Miu had said, and pushed off silently from the bank. The sun was already dropping behind the Theban mountains. I felt my own heart sinking too. Hidden in the mauve shadows beneath the cliffs were the bodies of

Tuthmosis's parents – King Amenhotep lying in his red sarcophagus waiting to journey to the Afterlife, and Queen Tiy, waiting for the Opening of the Mouth ceremony. And my own father? Was he there too? In one of the passageways, finding his way towards us?

I prayed with all my heart that it was so.

I looked back at Tuthmosis. 'How far will we go tonight?' I whispered.

'Beyond the outer city of Thebes.'

Beyond the outer city! It was a frightening thought. The furthest I'd ever gone was across the Great River to the western bank. Now I thought of Katep. Like him, I was travelling further and further away from everything I had ever known. What lay behind was gone for ever. It wouldn't do me any good to look back. But how could I look forward? What lay ahead was too unknown. I was caught in a time of nowhere. The thought numbed me into silence and made the paddles clumsy in my hands.

The breeze had died. In the slow silver light, the only sound came from the flap of the sail and the swish of our paddles, as we urged the boat forward against the smooth-running current. Now and again, the stillness was broken by the splash of a whiskered catfish as it broke the surface to catch a water-fly, or the flutter of wings as a surprised heron flew up from the reeds.

A sudden sound of oars behind us made my heart leap. In the purple dusk, I saw a dark red sail and the huge bulk of *Dazzling Aten*, its sharp prow slicing through the water, bearing down on us.

CHAPTER EIGHT

WOSRET

'They're after us! They know we've escaped. Ta-Miu must have told them!'

'Impossible! Ta-Miu would *never* reveal our secret.'

'Then why are we being followed?'

'Someone must have spotted us.'

'Paddle faster!'

'We can't out-row them! They've twenty oarsmen and a captain who knows no mercy.'

'Stop rowing then!'

'One moment you say paddle faster, the next you say stop rowing. Which do you want?'

I grabbed the girl's wig Tuthmosis had refused to wear. 'Put this on! Pull the tunic across your shoulder.

Quick! You *have* to be a girl now! It's our only hope. They're looking for a prince and a girl. Not two sisters. Don't speak! Don't let them hear your voice. I'll answer for both of us.'

The barge was gaining on us. While Tuthmosis arranged his wig and clothing I paddled closer to the reeds. If we were lucky they would pass without seeing us hidden between the papyrus. I turned to inspect Tuthmosis. He made a handsome peasant girl. His eyes challenged me to keep silent.

'Wrap something around your forehead so your eyes don't show,' is all I said.

Now the barge was so close its sails blocked the last pale light of the sky. With a shudder of horror, I made out the Highest of High Priests, Wosret, sitting under his canopy. Two slaves held flaming torches on either side of him. This journey had to be serious for him to travel by night. The captain stood in the prow holding a torch to light the way so the barge would not run into logs and floating papyrus and debris being swept down river.

We sat quietly, our paddles still, holding our breath. For a moment I thought they might pass, but the captain's hand went up. 'Hold your oars!' he shouted back to the men, then pointed. 'There's something out there! Between the papyrus alongside the bank.'

With a sudden swish all oars came up and the barge glided silently towards us. The captain leaned forward in the prow. His large chest gleamed in the torchlight and his fiery red hair teased out and lost its edge as it sprouted and tangled with his beard and made a huge lion's mane around his sweaty face.

'Who are you?' His voice boomed over the silent water like thunder.

'Two peasant girls, sir. Come from the Sophet Festival.' I did my best to put on a rough country accent and kept my head bowed to appear like a humble farm girl. I prayed Wosret would not come up to the prow as well. We were so low in the water that from where he was seated, his view of us was not face on.

The captain waved his torch above us. 'What are you doing out on the river at dusk? Are you not frightened of crocodiles?

'Crocodiles don't scare us sir!'

'Well they should, you foolish girl! Why are you returning so late?'

'We've come from the Sophet Festival, sir.'

'Yes,' he answered testily. 'You've said that!'

'Our dog has died. She was trampled underfoot in the crush at the Festival. We've come to offer her as a sacrifice to the great God Sobek. As you know, sir, it is said that whoever is devoured by the crocodile god, Sobek, is possessed for ever by divinity!'

There was a snigger from one of the oarsmen. 'A divine dog!'

'Well-spoken of the great God Sobek! How is it that you know so much of him?' The torchlight flickered across the captain's coarse features and wild mane as he waited for my reply.

I bit my lip. I was always saying too much! Speaking too freely! Why couldn't I hold my tongue?

'Captain!' Wosret called out impatiently from beneath the canopy, 'Enough of this time wasting! Hurry with your questioning. Make sure they are who they say they are. Then let's be on our way.'

'Yes, sir,' the captain nodded, as he peered across the water. 'So, where's your dog?'

Tuthmosis crouched forward and whispered under his breath. 'Tell him we've already thrown it overboard!'

'The dog is here, sir!'

'Idiot! What'll you do now?' Tuthmosis hissed.

The captain held the torch high. A path of gold rippled across to us. 'What are you whispering about? Where *is* the dog?'

I grabbed a skin Ta-Miu had given us, snapped the cord that bound it and gathered it up in my arms, holding it as if it had the weight of muscle and bone. 'Here, sir!'

'Well, girl – offer it to Sobek then! Throw it in!'

'Yes sir! But I don't know the proper incantations.'

'Say what you want. Just get on with it!'

'To the Great God Sobek. May he not crush two humble peasant girls between his mighty teeth. May he arise from the water and take our offering that we most humbly and earnestly—'

'Enough! Enough! Sobek has heard you! So have we all! Cast your dog before him now, without further preamble or speech making!'

I hurled the skin bundle into the water on the side closest to the reeds and watched the water take it, praying it wouldn't spread out and float towards their boat, into the path of the torchlight. For a moment it seemed to catch the current but then was trapped by a clump of reed. Before they could notice anything suspicious, I picked up my paddle and whacked it down hard and then called back to the captain, 'It wouldn't do for a dead dog to drift alongside the Royal Barge, sir!'

Suddenly Wosret appeared in the prow alongside the captain.

'Who is this girl? How does she know this is the Royal Barge?'

'I can . . .' I bit my lip. I had almost said the word *read*! But no peasant girl would be able to read. 'I can see by the red sail and the handsome decoration that, it *has* to be a boat of some importance!'

He stared at us across the water in silence. I held my breath and kept my head bowed. Next to me, so did Tuthmosis.

Then Wosret pointed at Tuthmosis. 'That one – your sister. She's a silent one!'

'She grieves, sir. The dog was her favourite pet.' I was glad the night air had turned my voice husky. Wearing a servant's wig and speaking with a deeper voice, I prayed Wosret wouldn't recognise me. Or Tuthmosis in his girl's tunic and wig.

'Where is your father that he allows two girls alone on the river at night?'

'Celebrating, sir! It's the Sophet Festival.'

The captain nodded. 'Drunk, probably! Eh?'

'Maybe so, sir. There's a new King to be celebrated, sir.' From beneath my wig I kept my eye on Wosret while I spoke.

'That we know, girl!'

I nodded but kept silent.

The captain held the lamp a little higher and then turned to Wosret. 'They're alone and fairly comely. Feisty, maybe? Should we take them on board? Two young girls might entertain the men. This being the Sophet Festival after all, sir?'

There was a cheer from the oarsmen. My heart seemed to stop beating in sudden terror. I felt Tuthmosis's fingers dig into my arm. No! I wanted to shout – No! No!

Wosret shook his head impatiently. 'The men need no distraction. We're wasting our time. Just find out what they know.'

My breath came out in a huge sigh.

The captain nodded, and then called down, 'We're on the lookout for two traitors. A prince and a young girl. Have you seen them come this way?'

I swallowed hard and tried to sound light-hearted. 'If we'd seen a prince, sir, we'd have followed him. We're poor peasant girls, sir. A prince would have done us well.'

The captain chuckled. 'Well, watch out for one. Be sure to report to an official if you come across a prince who limps.'

'A prince who limps, did you say? It wouldn't be the Crown Prince Tuthmosis, sir?'

Behind me, I heard Tuthmosis's sharp gasp.

The captain shook his head. 'What foolish girls you are, eh? Tuthmosis is dead! How else would his brother, Amenhotep, be King? It's another prince we search for.'

Wosret snapped his fingers at the captain and oarsmen. 'Let's waste no more time on these imbeciles! Darkness is descending. Row on! They can't have got far!'

We sat in silence after they passed, until their wake no longer washed against us and our boat finally stopped rocking and the night grew dark around us.

Finally Tuthmosis let out a deep sigh as if he had been holding his breath. 'That was stupid of you, Isikara.'

I found I was shivering. 'I hate him! I *loathe* Wosret!'

'But you didn't have to taunt him.'

'I wanted him to feel guilty!'

'A man like Wosret never feels guilty!'

'I had to say something! That man has killed my father! He has made him drink the poison cup.' Suddenly I could no longer hold in my tears.

98

'You don't know that for sure.'

'I *do* know! My father would've followed otherwise. Why else hasn't he? And why else would Wosret be out on the river looking for us at night? They've discovered my father replaced you. You heard Wosret! *They can't have gone far* . . . He knows! He's after us! And he's killed my father!'

'But you didn't have to pretend to throw the dog into the river! Now we've lost our blanket!'

'What?' I gasped. 'You arrogant, unfeeling brute! What do blankets matter when I've lost my *father*? There were *two* in the bundle.' I hurled another skin into his lap. 'You didn't think Ta-Miu expected us to share a blanket, did you?'

We stared back at one another unflinchingly. Then he turned abruptly and reached into the woven basket and plucked out a flask of sweet fig wine and pulled the stopper with a sharp plop and drank some. He held out the flask towards me. 'Here! Have some of this. You're not yourself and neither am I. Remember,' his voice dropped lower, 'I've *also* lost a parent.'

I eyed him angrily. 'It's not the same for you!'

'How do you know?'

'Because you're a prince!'

99

'Do princes not have feelings?'

I glared straight back at him. How could he of all people, with his cold indifference, know how I truly felt? I wanted to thump my fists against his chest. Instead I snatched the flask from him, took a quick gulp and almost choked at its strength.

'There's nothing wrong with me! It's *you* who is strange!' I snapped as I wiped my mouth with the back of my hand. 'I'm fine!' But suddenly I felt my stomach heave and before I could help myself, I was spewing over the side of the boat.

'Isikara?' He put a hand on my shoulder.

I shrugged it off. 'I'm fine! Just . . .'

'Yes?'

'Leave me alone.' I bent over the side of the boat and vomited into the water again. 'I'm just . . .' I shook my head. 'I'm just angry and . . .'

'And what?'

'Scared . . . maybe?'

He sat back in the boat and began to laugh.

I glanced over my shoulder at him. 'What? Curse you, Tuthmosis! At a time like this, you laugh?'

'Sorry. But I never thought I'd hear you admit to that.'

'To what?'

'Being scared.'

'And I thought I'd never hear you say sorry!' I snapped at him.

'We could've been killed then. No one would've known. Our bodies thrown to the crocodiles in the darkness. We'd have disappeared for ever!'

'So?' I eyed him.

He was looking at me strangely. 'But we weren't, were we?'

I shook my head.

'We weren't – because of *your* resourcefulness and your bravery! You managed to bluff Wosret! You outwitted him. That's something to celebrate. We should drink a toast! We've seen the last of him. The last – until I've gathered my army against him.'

'We'll *never* see the last of him!' The bile rose up in my throat again.

Tuthmosis must have seen my despair, because he reached out and touched my shoulder. 'Don't say that. What lies ahead will be different. But we'll live the days as they come. My father's kingdom stretches as far as the Second Cataract of the Great River. Beyond that in the land of Kush, we'll be free of Wosret. I'll gather an army to fight him. To fight for my crown.'

I looked back at him and willed myself to believe what he said.

We pulled the boat up between the papyrus reeds and spread the skin blanket on top of some flattened grass under a grove of palm trees. Then we ate the millet cake and slices of roast fowl Ta-Miu had provided. A smell of wood-smoke and a sound of far-off drums and celebrations drifted back to us from Thebes. I stood up and took some smooth, flat pebbles and flicked them angrily, one after another, across the water so that they skimmed the surface and jumped like agitated flying fish.

Even Katep would have been impressed with my skill. But if Katep had been here, I might not have been in this mess.

Eventually, even the frogs fell silent and darkness came down like a cloak. Tuthmosis pulled the skin around us and soon he was breathing deeply. We lay together with our bodies not touching and I felt for the knots on my bracelet and prayed to Hathor for protection. Then I asked for forgiveness as well, for calling Tuthmosis an arrogant, unfeeling brute.

I must have fallen asleep because later something

woke me. There was a swish of grass and the sound of someone treading very quietly. A huge, dark shape was crouching in the grass. Then I heard a snuffle and the tear of grass being pulled and snapped and a deep rumble of guts and a foul smell. It was a hippopotamus! And we were lying right in its path! I felt my skin go clammy. I could hardly breathe as I nudged Tuthmosis.

'Tuthmosis!' I whispered, close to his ear.

'Wh . . . what?' he turned over grumpily.

'Ssshh!'

There was silence as the hippopotamus stopped eating. I imagined the ears swivelling and twitching around to catch the sound of us. One snap of those huge jaws, and we'd be done for!

Then the sound of grass being pulled and snapped started up again.

'There's a hippopotamus. Next to us.'

'Lie still.' He whispered in my ear. 'They have poor eyesight.'

I lay rigid with my arms stiffly at my sides, too terrified to even breathe, and prayed the grass we were lying on wasn't as sweet-tasting as the grass further down towards the river.

'Tuthmosis . . .?' I whispered later when I sensed

103

the creature had moved further away. There was no reply, except the sound of even breathing.

All thought of sleep had gone. I lay with my eyes wide open and watched the moon come up, a little fuller now than the fine thread I'd seen on the morning that marked the ritual of crocodile bathing at the Temple of Sobek. I had lost track of the days. But one thing I *was* sure of – Tuthmosis was *not* going to be the best of protectors.

I felt for my moonstone amulet and prayed to Hathor again – this time to ward off the evils, not just for my sake, but for his sake as well. Then I searched the sky to find the stars that outlined Orion, the Hunter with his bow and arrow. Katep's constellation. I willed Katep to be searching the stars as well. To be looking up from the desert in Sinai and to be thinking of me. I thought of my father's words, *If you've learned the constellations and the stars, then wherever you are in the world, you'll never be lost.*

I held onto that thought. I would *not* be lost! Not even in spirit. As long as the hunter, Orion, was in the sky, I was safe. This was just as well, because we were to come across the Royal Barge again sooner than expected.

CHAPTER NINE

GOD OF THE BLUE LOTUS ... NEFERTEM

We journeyed upriver, driven by the steady wind that blew at our back and a fear that never left us. We were constantly alert and watchful. The thought that at any moment we might suddenly come across Wosret and his soldiers in some village upstream or some lonely bend of river kept us not just vigilant but uneasy.

Our journey took us past clusters of villages hidden between tufts of palms, the mud and palm-beam houses almost invisible in their surroundings – their walls the exact colour of the ground on which they stood. In the fields men hoed in preparation for the floods and along the banks women washed tunics and spread them over the reeds to dry.

The river was wide. A broad expanse of blue that made our boat seem all the smaller and gave us the chance to give other boats a wide berth. We sat low in the water and kept close to the reeds. Crocodiles slithered from the banks with a splash when we came upon them unexpectedly. But for the most part they lay still as stone, their mouths open and their throats exposed to the sun. Bubbles on the water and a flick of ears gave us warning of hippopotami lurking beneath the surface. When they rose, with snorting, angry grunts, we gave them space and sailed quickly past.

Occasionally we came upon men in small reed boats like ours, with plaited fishing nets and spears, who waved from a distance but took little notice of us. The larger vessels were too intent on their passage of plying grain and oil and cloth to the Temples along the river to take note of us.

Food was no problem. The reeds were teeming with every type of waterfowl – ducks, wild geese, herons, crakes and waders that had nests hidden between the papyrus stems. Tuthmosis was good with a throwstick and spear. Here and there we pulled ashore in smaller villages and traded the mullet and catfish we caught for dates and honey and barley bread.

Once we came to a village of linen dyers where

the river ran red with their dye. Sometimes there were markets where linen and wool weavers and craftsmen made cloths, pottery bowls, leather sandals and copper pots, and merchants offered cones of salt, dried fish, combs of ivory and tortoiseshell and fly-whisks made from giraffe tails, while market attendants walked about with baboons on leashes trained to catch thieves.

The baboons barked and bared their teeth and made me uneasy and nervous of being found out. For the most part we avoided these busy places, where there was more chance of our identity being discovered by Wosret's spies. We stopped on the outskirts of quieter villages to cook our fish and make meals of chickpeas and lentils stewed with garlic and onion over a fire, while the sounds of children playing late into the night came to us under the stars.

In the boat Tuthmosis wore only his wrap and refused to dress disguised as a girl, despite my arguments. But amongst people he put on his girl's wig and drew a cloth around his face to keep his eyes in shadow, so their colour was hidden. We kept to the story – we were sisters sailing south to discover another life. For the most part Tuthmosis remained silent and I spoke for both of us. We drew no attention to ourselves and in our rough clothes and crudely woven boat, it wasn't difficult to convince people of our peasant stock.

From carefully listening to gossip, we tracked the route of Wosret travelling ahead of us, and learned he was no favourite of the people.

'*Dazzling Aten* passed along the river here.'

'The Highest of High Priests came at dusk. His soldiers moved through our village, eating our food, drinking our barley beer and threatening anyone who opposed them.'

'I heard the commotion from the fields. They held my wife and children captive, searching through the rooms of our house, ransacking our belongings.'

'What were they searching for?'

'A prince, they say. But they wouldn't name him. Some say it could even be Tuthmosis.'

'Tuthmosis? But is he not dead?'

'Yes. But so sudden a death seems very strange.'

'Did they find this prince?'

'They found nothing!'

'Have they returned this way?'

'Not that I know. But they could've passed at night while we slept, and returned to Thebes.'

And since we heard no further stories, nor caught

sight of the Royal Barge the further south we sailed, we finally came to believe that this is what had happened. Wosret had returned to Thebes. And we began to feel a little less fearful.

Tuthmosis eyed me as we sat in our boat between the reeds one day. 'It's good you're accurate with your throwstick. You hunt like a boy!'

I smiled at the admiration of his glance. In the base of the boat lay two waterfowl. Secretly, I was pleased with my stealth. I had come upon a pair of shy, green herons – the female on her nest and the male fussing next to her. Before they could fly up, I had aimed the throwstick and stunned both birds with one throw. Silence and stealth. Days spent on the river with Katep had taught me this.

I shrugged. 'It takes a good stick. My brother, Katep, carved mine from the rib of a hippopotamus. It's easy to handle. Perfectly balanced. Deadly accurate. See – he made carvings on it of a jackal and a snake to invoke their power and help me throw accurately.'

Tuthmosis laughed as he ran his fingers over the carvings. 'It's not the jackal and the snake which are accurate, it's *you!*'

109

I felt the blush rise to my cheeks, turned my face so he wouldn't see and fumbled with untying the sail, my hands made clumsy by his compliment.

Tuthmosis was in playful mood. As soon as he stepped ashore, he began gathering poppies and cornflowers and sprigs of willow and wild olive.

'What are you doing?'

'Wait and see.' He sat with the flowers and sprigs in his lap, first cutting a long length of papyrus stem and tying the end pieces together to make a circle. Then, using thin strands of the papyrus head, he tied and wove individual leaves and flowers onto the ring in rows. His hands worked easily, deftly twisting olive leaves and willow salix and the heads of wild celery and sage with blue cornflowers and red poppies.

I laughed at his earnestness. 'Where did you learn to make flower collars?'

He glanced up and smiled. 'From the Palace serving girls. They sat in the gardens weaving collars for each other.' He made some final adjustments and carefully placed it over my head and arranged it across my shoulders. Then he snapped his fingers. 'I forgot! There must be perfume as well.' He snatched up two blue lotus lilies from the river's edge and stuck them into the collar.

'There!' He stood back, smiling. I wasn't sure if he was admiring his work or looking at me. 'A Temple goddess.'

I could hardly return his look. I knew I was blushing. To hide my confusion, I pulled a lily from the necklace and placed it behind his ear. 'You must wear one as well!'

There he stood, handsome as Nefertem, looking strong enough to ride the back of a lion. Royal breeding showed in the way he held his body and in the tilt of his head on his broad shoulders. He was handsome without seeming to know it. The heady perfume of the lilies made me giddy. Without realising, I spoke the words aloud. 'Nefertem – God of the Blue Lotus.'

Our eyes met. His truly blue. As blue as the lotus flowers he'd picked. I looked away hurriedly.

Afterwards, he built a small fire with reed and driftwood while I plucked the two waterfowl in silence, then split them open to scrape out the gall and innards and wrapped them in lotus leaves and laid them in the embers. We ate in silence, listening to

111

the frogs and picking the meat off the bone. Then I lay looking up at the stars, with the strong perfume of the flowers about my neck wafting over me.

Tuthmosis stretched out next to me with his head cupped in his hands and began talking. 'I slept like this in the desert, when I was a child.'

I smiled into the darkness. 'Don't be silly! Princes don't sleep on the ground. They sleep on gold beds in palaces.'

'I did! I slept on the ground. You must believe me! I went hunting with my father. His days were free of military skirmishes then. Syria, Palestine and Babylon were already his dominions. He had plenty of time for hunting.'

'And ...?' I was thirsty for the sound of his voice.

'We raced in two-horse chariots over the flood-plains, a charioteer at the reins, the wheels of the cart careering across the sand, my father wearing the blue, gold-studded Khepresh Warrior Crown, targeting antelope and ibex. As we gained on them my father would draw his bow and add to his tally. Fierce lions and leopards too. He hunted them all.'

Tuthmosis himself grew fierce with his words. 'You saw the skins on the floor of my mother's chamber. In ten years my father felled more than a hundred lions! He wore the skins as cloaks to show his greatness. So all would know his strength and courage!'

I turned on my side and rested my head on my elbow to look at him. 'And you . . .? Did you hunt well?'

'My father never gave me the chance to test my skills. I stood at his side while he shot the arrows. When we returned and the pace was slow, he allowed the charioteer to hand me the reins. That's what I liked best. But I never seemed able to prove myself to my father.'

'How so?'

'Everything he did, whether it was hunting lion or building monuments, was to demonstrate his greatness. The lavish banquets, the mammoth statues guarding his Mortuary Temple, the Palace, the Temple at Luxor inscribed with his name – all were intended to overawe.'

Tuthmosis sat up abruptly and raked some life into the fire. Suddenly there was a bitter tone to his voice.

'My brother, sisters and I grew up not wanting for anything. Our playthings were made of gold inlaid with precious stones. We had giraffes and cheetahs for playmates. Monkeys were trained to retrieve fruit for us from the highest branches of our orchards. Slaves stood by to attend to our every need.'

He broke a stick with a sharp snap and laid it across the flames. 'My father was generous but in exchange he wanted absolute power.'

I glanced across at him. In the firelight his eyes sparked. He was quiet for a long time, as if searching for the right words.

'Yes . . .?' I urged.

He shrugged. 'His power sapped the foundations of everything. Nothing I did, whether it was driving a chariot well or showing I was an expert marksman, ever drew him to me. In his eyes, I was nothing. Especially after the accident.'

I stole another sideways glance. He stared past me into the fire as if he'd forgotten I was there. 'The accident . . .?'

'On a hunting expedition I fell from the chariot when the wheel hit a loose stone. My leg caught in the spokes as it rolled over me. They thought my leg might have to be amputated. The bone was broken and the flesh wouldn't heal. But I eventually recovered and have walked with a limp ever since.'

He turned and searched my face as if looking for some answer there. Then he shrugged. 'My father always wanted perfection. He chose my younger brother, his namesake – Amenhotep, as his favourite then.'

The next morning we set out early, hugging the bank of the river. There had been days without incident. I found myself humming softly as we sailed. I felt light and easy. Free of the threat of Wosret.

My mind was far away, when a sudden glimmer caught my eye.

A mirage was rising above the reeds in a bend in the river up ahead. A tall, hazy shape that shimmered in the heat, as if overlaid with gold gauze. A shape with a mast and a high, golden prow.

It came downstream directly towards us in the glittering, morning light, its red sails slack, driven forward by the fast downstream current and the strength of its many oarsmen.

I sat like a snake charmed into stillness by its master. I knew there was something we should do. But the barge had appeared so silently and unexpectedly in such a deserted part of the river that my body was numb.

I heard Tuthmosis's sharp intake of breath behind me. 'It can't be!' His voice was stiff with outrage. But

115

when I turned, I saw him sitting equally mesmerised.

The hiss of water against the barge's prow and the beat of oars brought me back to my senses. 'We can't fool them a second time. There's no protection of darkness now. They'll easily recognise us. We have to do something!'

'But what?'

'Hide before we're spotted.'

'There's nowhere to hide, except under the water.'

'Quick! That's it! Take a hollow reed to breathe through and slip beneath the water.'

Tuthmosis frowned.

'It'll work! I've done it before. My brother and I used to play this game. We took turns to see how long we could stay under the water.' I snapped a hollow reed and passed it to Tuthmosis. 'Here! Hurry!'

'What about crocodiles?'

I glanced around quickly and shook my head. 'None!' I didn't tell him that when I'd played this game with Katep one of us had always kept watch. I slipped over the side of the boat, ducked down and prayed to Sobek to spare us from crocodiles in exchange for all the times Katep and I had fed his sacred beasts.

I thrust the end of my reed upwards and sucked hard. No air came. For a moment, my heart raced. The reed was blocked. But there was no time to surface and choose another. Panic was setting in. I blew hard and dislodged whatever was stuck inside it. Under the murky water I saw Tuthmosis holding his reed tightly in his mouth, his eyes wide open and staring back at me like two, silvery-blue fish.

There was a muffled swish of oars and a surge of water as the barge beat down on us. My heart was drumming in my head. Or was it the noise of the barge? I held my breath. Would they notice our boat lodged between the reeds? Its fibres were so water-soaked that it floated low in the river. It had bleached to a dull grey colour during the journey and its woven strands were beginning to unravel. I prayed they would mistake it for debris swept down by the floods.

Yet at any moment I expected to hear the rapid hiss of the flax rope and the splash and muffled thump of a heavy harpoon anchor. Expected to see the dark hull at my side and to be yanked up by the arm.

I wasn't getting enough air. My lungs were bursting. I tried to even my breathing. I saw Tuthmosis trying to nod reassuringly, and then he held his hand out with palm towards me as if telling me not to be in too much of a hurry.

We waited under the water for what seemed like

for ever. I strained my eyes for the shadow of the boat and my ears for the beat of oars. But this time it was truly only my heart I could hear thudding.

When we finally burst through the surface spitting the reeds from our mouths and gasping for a full, deep breath, the barge was nothing more than a golden dragonfly hovering in the heat haze, far in the distance downriver, heading back in the direction of Thebes at last.

I gulped another deep breath, and bellowed after them, 'Murderer! Vile murderer! You act divine. As untouchable as a god! But you're *not*! You *killed* my father, Wosret!'

Tuthmosis was silent as he held out his hand to help me from the water.

I brushed my cheeks angrily with the back of my hand, hoping the tears would mingle invisibly with river water and stood shivering, even though the sun was hot against my skin.

Then Tuthmosis picked a single blue lotus lily and pushed it into the collar of flowers that still lay in wet, bedraggled strands around my shoulders. He gave a slight bow. His mouth curved up into a broad smile but his eyes were serious. 'To Kara – most supreme waterfowl hunter and deviser of untold tricks!'

As I looked back at him, I saw the smile catch his eyes as well. He leaned forward and wiped a piece of reed or fleck of mud from my face with his thumb. For a moment his hand lingered against my cheek. Then he tipped my chin upwards and brought his head closer and kissed my lips. I'm not sure how long his mouth stayed against mine, but it was enough for me to feel the warmth and touch of his lips long afterwards.

That night, as I settled down in a hollow in the sand next to him with the canopy of stars as our tent, I found myself raising my fingers to touch my lips as if to stop them tingling ... or perhaps to stop them smiling.

CHAPTER TEN

MIRAGES OF WATER RISE UP LIKE WAVES

We came eventually to a lonely part of the river with nothing but high, desert sand dunes to our western side and dry, barren, stony ground to the east. Both riverbanks were desolate and empty without palm trees, villages, or children tending goats and playing in the mud. The landscape was harsh and arid and unwelcoming.

The following morning I woke stiff and chilled next to the huge dunes that rose up clear and cold, and almost blue in the early light. There was a smell of wood-smoke. Tuthmosis was already crouching over some embers, stirring them back to life. I moved closer and spread my hands out to warm them. The dunes began to glow and take on the colour of the rising sun, as he handed me a gourd of water he had scooped up from the river. Then he fumbled in his girdle bag and held out some dry pieces of millet bread and a few olives.

'I saved them from the last village in case you might be hungry.'

I couldn't help smiling into the gourd. 'You're suited to the life of a nomad.'

Suddenly I saw his face freeze.

I turned sharply and followed his gaze. A movement high up along the ridge of the nearest dune caught my eye.

Five men on camels were outlined in silhouette against the pale sky. For a moment they stood completely still and silent. I twisted my head from side to side to scan the landscape. But there was no escape. They had seen us and it was too late for Tuthmosis to slip on his girl's tunic and wig.

'Bind your head at least!' I hissed.

Just then the sun tipped the horizon and the men began riding slowly down the slope towards us. As the rays caught them, they appeared to be dressed in brilliant metallic mesh woven with gold brocade that shimmered with every slow, tantalising step. But as they drew closer and closer, I saw the motley mix of clothes they wore – layers of bleached and tattered linen with edges unravelling and cloth more patched than whole: sleeves that hung in tatters round their wrists and head-cloths that blew and unfurled in the breeze in teased-out strips around their heads. They were bleached, weathered and worn to nothing but rags, bone and sinew – their dark faces scorched and lined from sun and wind, with tattoos marking their high cheeks.

Then I noticed something more fearful – the glint and flash of sunlight on metal. An icy coldness raked through my flesh. The girdles around their waists were stuffed with weapons – jewelled daggers and adzes and bronze sickle swords – and, slung across their backs were enormous bows and dark hide quivers bulging with arrows.

I had never seen desert nomads but instinctively I knew these were the Medjay – expert bowmen who roamed the deserts, trading and slitting throats and impaling people for whatever price or prize.

'Stay silent! Let me speak,' Tuthmosis hissed as he straightened up to meet them.

Their leader stopped short of us. His face, half shadowed by his head-cloth, was harsh and his eyes dark and unfathomable. Up close I saw the strong jaw-line and high tattoo-marked cheeks and noticed the boots sticking out from under his wind-torn cloak. His cloak and head-cloth were worn to threads but his desert boots, as high as his calves, were made of strong leather and stitched in an intricate design.

The other men were silent. Their reins lay loosely in their hands and their eyes watched fiercely.

The leader's dark eyes flicked over us. 'What do you want here?'

'We're sailing to beyond the first and second cataract.'

'The first cataract is a long way off. The second even further!'

'We know,' Tuthmosis answered, although I wasn't sure he *did* know.

'Where are you from?'

'From . . .?'

'Yes. From.' The man stared back.

'A village downriver—'

'Tuthmosis is the King's son,' I interrupted. If he was truly a Medjay, for our own protection it might be well to tell him we were powerful. Then I bit my lip, as I caught Tuthmosis's stunned scowl.

The man turned and looked me up and down with

the dark eye of someone used to assessing goods to trade in. Then he leaned back on his camel and laughed. But it was a laugh without any mirth. More a sneer. 'And you're the King's daughter?'

Tuthmosis broke in. 'My sister's confused. We've been travelling a long while. The heat of the sun has touched her. We're peasants.'

'What are peasants doing so far from their village? Have you broken the law? Are you fleeing?'

'We told you. We're going further up the river,' Tuthmosis answered.

'To what purpose?'

Tuthmosis was silent.

The man narrowed his eyes as he looked at me and then turned to the men. 'Perhaps the girl speaks the truth. Perhaps they're *not* peasants.' The other men looked on with hard, expressionless faces. 'We'll take them. We could sell them. The Pharaoh's son would fetch a good price. And the Pharaoh's daughter—?'

'No . . . no!' I interrupted. 'My brother is right. I'm confused. And I'm certainly *not* the Pharaoh's daughter.'

He turned back to me and spoke slowly, as if explaining to a child. 'I know that.' He held my eyes.

'Because the new Pharaoh, Amenhotep, is just a boy. He has no daughter!'

'The new Pharaoh?' I stared back at the man. How could he know about Tuthmosis's brother already? How had he heard the news on the edge of the desert so far from Thebes? What *else* did he know?

He smiled as he saw my look. 'We have spies. Perhaps there's more money to be made by selling both of you back to the authorities.' He looked between us with an eyebrow raised, as if he expected an answer. 'Perhaps to the High Priests of Thebes? I hear they are keen to find a certain boy and girl who have escaped.'

Without warning he reached down swiftly and yanked me up onto his camel by my left arm and swung me across the animal's back in front of him. And even though I squirmed and fought and tried to pull away, he clutched me and held me tightly against his chest to prevent me from slipping free.

The camel protested at the extra burden with sounds like a braying donkey that had broken its leg. This spurred the group into action. One man beat his camel to make it kneel, then reached across and pulled Tuthmosis onto the front, another scooped up our skin blanket with the tip of his sickle sword and flung it across to Tuthmosis. Another reached down and with a few swift, scything movements sliced our boat apart so that nothing was left but a heap of debris stranded on the sand.

Amidst a hubbub of braying camels, the men dug their heels into their animals and urged them around. Before I could exchange more than a look with Tuthmosis, we were moving in single file up the dune, the leader up front with me held tightly against him and my legs dangling over the side of his camel and Tuthmosis riding somewhere behind.

I felt the roughness of the Medjay's rags against my arms and his torn head-veil whipping against my face in the wind as we topped the crest of the dune. Ahead of us there was nothing but endless desert.

He pulled off a strip of roughly woven wool from his body and handed it to me. 'You'll need this for protection against the sun and sandstorms.'

The strip felt greasy in my hands and smelled suffocatingly of goat. But I wrapped it around my head and face to protect me from the glare. From a peep-hole in the swaddle, all I could see were his sinewy arms and his grimy hands with dirt-lined nails as he held the camel reins and at the same time clutched firmly onto me.

The heat drew a suffocating stench of camel, wood-smoke and sweat from his body. But as we rode into the blinding desert, I was conscious not just of the smell of him, but of the sickle sword that kept bumping against my thigh and the bulge of the dagger that pressed hard against the small of my back.

If only I had paid heed to my father's words. If only I had held my tongue, they might've believed we were peasants. Was Tuthmosis silently cursing me? I twisted and turned to try and get a glimpse of him but the Medjay's arms entrapped me with as much force as the jaws of a crocodile.

We rode in silence with the sun beating down. I'd never ridden a camel before. Its gait was clumsy. I discovered in time that it had three ways of walking – a stumbling short stride like the rolling of a small boat on a choppy river; a longer stride which seemed to dislocate every bone in my body and a sudden, jerky gallop that felt as frightening as instant death. All of them were unsettling.

There was no way of knowing what distance we were covering. In the middle of the day we rested in a narrow passage of shade cast by a wind-worn outcrop of rock. The water the Medjay offered from leather skins that hung from their camels' necks was warm and tasted of goat. I glanced across at Tuthmosis, trying to read the message in his eyes but we were silenced by the men whenever we tried to speak.

In the middle of the afternoon, a murky cloud like a dark swarm of locusts gathered along the horizon. The camels became restless and the men wound their scarves tighter around their faces and turned their backs to the dark horizon. A hush fell, silent as a dead man's heart.

I peered out from beneath my swaddle as the dark cloud became a huge solid wall of dust and sand rolling towards us. As the wind gusted harder and harder, so the ragged outlines of the men seemed to be unfurling – their clothes, the torn head-veils, the edges of their tunics, unravelling – their shapes disappearing in the haze. Bent over their camels in the murky light, they were ghostly apparitions. I lost sight of Tuthmosis.

Then, with a howl like a raging animal, the storm of dust wrapped itself around us and the world turned dark. In terror I buried my head into the Medjay's shoulder and heard him laugh deep against my body.

Sand stung my arms and legs and my throat choked and my eyes were blinded. Against his chest, I heard the sound of his heart close to my ear. A sound that should have been comforting – but instead was terrifying. Yet I knew that had he not dug his fingers into my flesh and pinned me against him, I would have blown away.

CHAPTER ELEVEN

ANOUKHET

The storm blew itself out some time in the night while we clung to our camels. Somewhere in the midst of it I must have dozed. It was the complete silence that startled me from sleep. The desert stretched endlessly to the horizon, rippled as the surface of a river and completely unrecognisable. Strange shapes of rock and bones lay exposed and sand dunes stood where none had existed before.

We had been riding a long time when I spotted a dark green speck emerge in the middle of the blinding sand ahead. I was sure the sun had made me delirious. But it grew larger and larger until shapes of trees appeared and shimmered and jumped in the haze.

Spurred on by a sense of water, the camels kicked up sand and began to gallop. The Medjay leader gripped tightly on the reins to keep his animal under control while I was jostled and juggled about, with foaming spittle flying past my face, terrified I would fall under the huge, pounding, leathery feet.

Children and chickens scattered from beneath us and dogs barked all around as we rode between tall, feathery palm trees heavy with dates, and spreading acacias and low striped tents with sides tied up on stakes, exposing shadowy, mysterious interiors.

The camels laid back their ears and brayed and raised frothing lips to show their teeth, snapping in displeasure as the men struggled to halt them and prodded them into kneeling positions. The Medjay leader called out to some boys to unload the bags and bundles.

In the midst of all the noise and movement, I sat senseless, unable to move. He reached up, clasped me by the waist and swung me down, away from the snapping teeth of his camel. For a moment both his hands still held me. Then I pulled free of him, brushed the slimy camel spit from my face with the back of my arm, and ripped the ragged goat-skin scarf from my head. He laughed as he turned and walked away towards a tent the other men had entered.

The contrast between the desert and the oasis was beyond belief. In an instant we had moved from a world of blinding, blistering heat into a cool, green space, dappled and dancing with sunlight and shadow. It was like being trapped inside a glinting piece of dark emerald stone.

Alongside some rocks, a spring of water bubbled up from beneath the sand to form a pool where women with their faces and arms wrapped in linen were collecting water in terracotta jars. Peacocks strutted between them bringing their own glimmer of green to this shaded space.

Peacocks? How was it possible?

Tuthmosis was next to me. I caught his eye but we were both too exhausted to speak. People gathered, disturbed by the commotion, and stood at a distance and stared. A little boy touched my hand curiously but was scolded by his mother and shooed back to a tent. The women appeared to be discussing us. When one of them came forward with a gourd of water, I pulled it to my lips so eagerly that the water splashed and spilled onto the sand.

In the shadow of a tent, I saw a girl standing with her hand resting up against the tent pole, the other on her hip, staring straight at us. She was tall, loose-limbed, dark-skinned and exotic-looking. She wore a short boyish tunic and her hair was wild and free in a tousled mass of dark curls that fell around her face, instead of the carefully twisted and plaited wig-shapes worn in Thebes.

A woman clicked her fingers and said something to her. She tossed her head, turned and went inside, then brought out some bowls on a brass tray. She walked towards us with languid indifference as if no one could hurry her – her upright stance and the way she held her body making her seem defiant. Her tunic was rough and her boots were sturdy and made of leather held in place by straps around her ankles. Masses of silver bracelets shivered and shimmered against each other and an array of silver rings glinted on her fingers as she held out the tray.

The bowls were piled high with ripe dates, desert honeycomb and pomegranate seeds that glowed like garnets. There was a bowl of water for rinsing the hands, with a small piece of linen cloth next to it. Between the bowls lay a tiny spray of yellow mimosa flowers.

I crammed a piece of honeycomb into my mouth so quickly the honey had no time to drip, then I scooped up a handful of pomegranate seeds. The girl's dark amber eyes, deeper than the colour of the desert honey, seemed to challenge mine. She refused to look away and it was only when I felt the pomegranate seeds bursting against my tongue that she turned towards Tuthmosis.

I glanced across at him and wondered what he thought of her. She had brought the tray of food because she had been commanded. But the tiny sprig of mimosa on the tray, was that her doing?

Just then the Medjay leader strode out from the tent, followed by the other men. A hawk gripped the dusty linen cloak that covered his shoulder. It was tied to his wrist by a plait of fibre from a ring on its leg. A wild creature with a fierce eye and a screech that set my teeth on edge.

The man pushed the girl aside and shooed the women back. 'Enough! They're not guests!' Then he narrowed his eyes at us. 'It's been decided. You won't be tied up. You've seen the desert. You know what a journey across it is like. If you venture beyond this oasis, you'll soon be lost. If you try to escape, you'll never make it out of here alive. It's a brutal and savage death. Be warned!'

I glanced quickly at Tuthmosis and saw the

expression in his eyes. It was true. The Medjay had made a prison for us without stone walls. There was no way of knowing which direction to take back to the river. There were no paths across the shifting sands. The sandstorm had been treacherous. Death by thirst would be a horrible way to die! To be exposed to the burning sun, without water and shelter and no hopes of finding either, would be terrifying.

Tuthmosis eyed the leader. 'What's your plan for us?'

The man shrugged. 'You'll remain here until we find the right buyer. Someone who makes a good offer. Someone who wishes to return you to Thebes.'

'I thought the Medjay were against Thebes!'

'We're against anyone who wants to take away our freedom. But there are times when it's expedient to make friends with Thebes. She has conquered all her enemies right now, so there're not many bargains to be made. But the High Priests will be very interested to know we have captured the King's brother.'

'Tuthmosis's brother is *not* the true King!' I blurted out.

The man eyed me. 'At the Festival of Sophet, it was Amenhotep and not Tuthmosis who wore the Royal Atef Crown.'

So he knew everything!

'If we're not sold, what will you do with us?' Tuthmosis interrupted, without looking in my direction.

The leader appraised him with a sneer. 'A lame person is not much use to us. In our culture, people who are weak or old are left in the desert to die. There's no place for weakness in an oasis in the middle of the desert.'

He turned back to me and his eyes slid over me. 'But a girl is another matter ...' His voice was as silken, sweet and syrupy as the honey I had eaten, but his eyes were those of a falcon. A falcon watching its prey. The look sent a shudder through me. I couldn't speak. I could hardly breathe.

'Tonight we'll celebrate our safe return. The women will prepare a feast. There'll be music and dancing.' He turned and smiled at the girl. 'And Anoukhet will dance for us because I command it!'

She turned her head away with indifference, as if to study a bunch of dates that hung plump and orange between the fronds of a nearby palm. Just then a dog walked by with a monkey sitting balanced on its back.

'*Tsk tsk!*' The girl hissed softly through her teeth.

The monkey turned and leaped directly at her as if

to attack her face, but settled on her shoulder, as relaxed as if it had leaped onto a palm frond.

The girl straightened her back and tilted her chin slightly as she glanced across at me. Our eyes held for a short moment before she looked away again.

Anoukhet. So that was her name. But who was she? And where did she come from – this girl who was a dancer and a tamer of monkeys, who was so fiercely indifferent and yet was made to dance at the command of the leader?

CHAPTER TWELVE

SERPENTS OF SEQET

Be careful what you wish for. Wishes are poisonous and have a way of coming back to haunt you. They leave your lips as nothing more than vapour but once out in the air they've as much meaning as the most solemn curse about your neck. They burn your tongue and swell your throat as quickly and treacherously as venom from a cobra's bite.

They can *never* be undone.

When three bleating goats were brought by some children to be slaughtered for the feast that night, I thought of the sacrifices at the Temple, and of Katep, and remembered what I'd wished for the day he had left.

I had wished my life would change! But I hadn't dreamed it would change so much for the worse. This was all my own doing.

The throats of the three goats were quickly slit and the blood collected in bowls, then the bodies skinned and chopped and added to pots boiling over a crackling fire. Women were chopping onions and garlic, grinding fragrant leaves of rosemary and crushing cumin seeds and cinnamon sticks in a mortar to flavour the stew. Others were straining fermented barley beer into large terracotta jars.

I was made to work alongside some girls grinding flour and preparing loaves. Dogs squabbled around our feet for bits of bone and entrails. Children started a game of boisterous wrestling between us and laughter gusted around, as the women sweated and worked and cast sidelong glances at me. Peacocks, frightened into the trees by the commotion, screeched and added their own cacophony to the day.

Tuthmosis was nowhere to be seen. It was strange to be separated from him. Then Anoukhet appeared and set to silently kneading dough alongside me. Her bracelets chased back and forth along her arms as she worked. Her monkey perched in a palm tree near by.

After a while she whispered, 'He knows everything.

He knows exactly who you both are. He'll be ruthless about selling you back to Thebes when the time comes. It's no use staying here. Your only chance is to escape!'

I stopped and stared at her in confusion while the girls around us giggled and chatted. Flour had settled on her eyelashes and powdered them white, and there was a smear of dough across her cheek, but her expression was serious.

'Keep working!' she hissed. 'Don't draw attention to what I'm telling you.'

'We can never escape. It's too dangerous. How would we go?'

'By camel. It's the only way.'

'But we don't know the desert.'

'There's an old camel tender here. He knows his time is up. They'll put him out in the desert soon to die. So he has every reason to leave. He'll take us. He knows the way.'

'Us?'

'I'm coming with you.'

'Why?'

'This place is a nest of *scorpions*.' She hissed the word.

I gave her a sidelong glance.

'The Medjay are scorpions! Fast, unpredictable, poisonous! And every bit as deadly! They bury themselves in the sands of the desert and shelter under rocks, waiting to do evil. They're the most dangerous inhabitants of this earth. Serpents of the Underworld.'

She quickly drew a wedjat eye into the flour with her elbow to ward off evil. 'Do you know the legend of the Scorpion Goddess?'

I thought of Katep amongst the scorpions of Sinai. 'Yes – Seqet. She walks with the scorpion on her head and opens throats to breathe. She allows us to live.'

'But also to *die*! She can paralyse throats. She's a dangerous goddess. She protects but also punishes with her scorpion arrows. Her burning wrath causes death. Her scorpions are vicious. The Medjay are just as vicious. Don't be fooled by them. They strike when you least expect. They're a plague on this earth.'

She spat on the ground. 'Naqada is the worst scorpion of all!'

'Naqada?'

'The leader. He would kill you if it paid him more to do so. He is ruthless. He has trained his hawk to peck out people's eyes. If you see someone blind in the oasis, it's because of his hawk. Naqada is as evil as Apep!'

141

My mouth turned dry. It was a name that should *never* be uttered. God of Evil and Destruction. God of Chaos. Every day he tried to swallow the Sun. I shuddered. 'I beg you . . . don't! Don't give the Evil One power by saying his name! The world will be plunged into darkness. I know about the gods. I'm a priest's daughter.'

She stopped kneading for a moment and looked at me. 'I know. But your father has disappeared.'

'How do you know?'

'I watch and listen to what's spoken.'

'Then you *must* have news of him.'

'He hasn't been seen since the embalming of Queen Tiy.'

'The Highest of High Priests is worse than Naqada.'

'Like must be fought with like. Every day I make an effigy of a scorpion out of beeswax. The sting of a bee against the sting of a scorpion. I leave it out in the sun on the burning sand so it will melt to nothing, in the hope that Naqada's power will also disappear.'

'Has it?'

She shook her head. 'With each new dawn, Naqada's power is restored, and I must make a fresh effigy. I'm running out of precious wax. The only way to overcome Naqada is to escape him! I've been waiting my chance. With you and Tuthmosis and the old camel tender, we'll manage it.'

'You'll leave your family?'

'I've none. Naqada captured me as a child and brought me here from Nubia.'

I shook my head. Her plan seemed unthinkable.

'We *have* to!' she hissed urgently. 'It's the only way. We must leave before he strikes. Once he has someone interested in buying both of you, he'll guard you as closely as his hawk guards him. If he can't find a buyer to take you back to Thebes, he might do a deal with Wosret and kill you himself – for a price, of course! Whatever happens, neither of you will come out of this alive. You know too much. The High Priests don't want Tuthmosis claiming his rightful throne.'

She was shaping the dough so vigorously the charms on her bracelets in the shape of small creatures – frogs, scarabs, dragonflies, scorpions, bees and turtles – jangled against each other. She was slapping it into shape . . . as if the dough was all she cared about. But her breathlessness betrayed her. And soon the loaves would be lined up and ready for the baking ovens. The opportunity for talking would be over.

'What must we do?'

'We have to act quickly,' she whispered. 'Leave arrangements to me. The camel tender is ready to set off whenever I say. Tonight, while the feasting takes place, be sure to store some food for the journey. Dates, fruit, olives and nuts – whatever you can lay your hands on. Steal a saddlebag to carry it in. Bring a cloak or skin to wrap around you at night. And fill any water-skins you find. Tell Tuthmosis to do the same. Be sure to warn him, this is our *only* chance. When we leave will depend on how lively the celebration gets. Don't drink any wine or barley beer. No matter what. The stuff they make here is strong and potent. Stay alert. When I give the signal, it'll be time to go.'

I nodded and swallowed. Her plan was drastic, her words dire. It was hard to know whether to trust her, but if we didn't, all we could do was stay in the oasis and await our fate. We had already forfeited so much. To escape and find our way through the desert seemed less dangerous.

CHAPTER THIRTEEN

THE SEVEN RIBBONS OF HATHOR

Later, when the shadows lengthened, huge fires were lit and burning braziers placed along the pathways. I wandered between the tents on the outskirts of the oasis, searching for Tuthmosis, and found my hand suddenly grasped by Anoukhet.

She pulled me quickly towards a tent and lowered the flap. It was hung with coloured cloth and spread with woven rugs. Her monkey lay curled up on a goat-skin in a dark corner. Thick goat-skins were strewn everywhere and carved tables inlaid with ivory and mother-of-pearl held glass flasks, terracotta bowls and alabaster jars.

145

It seemed elaborate and luxurious for the tent of a slave girl.

'Have you told Tuthmosis yet?' she whispered in the half darkness.

I shook my head. 'I can't find him.'

'They're purposely keeping you apart, so you can't plot anything. *I'll* discover where they've sent him and tell him our plan.'

'Be careful of how you persuade him.'

'Why?'

I shrugged. 'Tuthmosis is a king's son. He's not used to taking orders.'

Anoukhet laughed as she lit an oil lamp. 'I need no warning. I'm not afraid of him.' The light caught a sparkle of mischief in her eyes. 'We must get ready for the celebration. They'll suspect something if we don't prepare ourselves.' She gave me a critical look. 'Your clothes are rough and dirty. Those sandals will be useless in the desert. You need leather boots like mine. We need to look like men, if we're come upon in the desert. And your wig is awful . . .' she pulled it from my head and examined the padding underneath '. . . and full of lice.'

I laughed at her outspokenness. 'It belonged to a servant. It was a disguise.'

146

'Wigs are useless in the desert. They're too hot to wear. You would do better to grow your hair long and let it fall naturally.'

I felt the short stubble of hair that had begun to grow on the journey. 'That's unheard of in Thebes! Normally my hair is shaved to the scalp.'

'We're far from Thebes now.' She was emptying water into a large terracotta basin. She removed a duck-headed stopper from a delicate, blue glass vial and tilted it carefully. A few drops of oil fell into the water. A sweet essence of rose petals, jasmine, oranges and almonds filled the air. Then she untied my robes and started to sponge me down. I felt like a small child being scrubbed by my mother.

Afterwards she made me sit and rubbed a thick lather of reed sap mixed with moss over my scalp and worked it in around my temples.

'Keep your eyes closed to stop the soapiness getting to them. This will rid you of any lice that may have escaped the wig and nestled in your own hair.'

Her bracelets of tiny creatures jingled and sang in my ears.

'Have you a cosmetic box for keeping oils for the journey? Galena and malachite pastes made with vege-table oils are needed for protection around the eyes.'

'I have turquoise paste.'

'*Turquoise* paste?' She paused in scrubbing. 'It's not a parade of beauty! Have you ever seen an animal that roams the wild with turquoise around its eyes? Or an antelope in the desert with turquoise eyes?'

Then she rubbed my head more vigorously as if trying to rid me not only of lice but also of my stupidity. 'No! A cheetah's eyes are lined with *black*. Gazelles have *dark* eyes. So must yours be! Black kohl, the grey paste of galena and the dark green of malachite around the eyelids are for *protection* in the desert . . . not just vanity!'

She scooped up water with impatience and let it run over my head and shoulders and then mopped me with a piece of linen. Then she tipped some oil from another vial into the palm of her hand to warm, before rubbing it across my back, shoulders and arms. Her hands worked roughly but expertly, her bracelets making their own music.

She laughed as I wrinkled my nose. 'It's palm oil perfumed with date flowers. You've been spoilt! The rose and almond oils of Thebes aren't freely available here! I used the little I had sparingly in your bathing water. But you'll get used to palm oil. Hold out your arms.'

148

She slipped a fresh robe over my head and brought the ends around my waist. It was long and finely pleated and fell from a knot tied on one shoulder. She shrugged as I examined the finely woven cloth. 'You can put on a man's tunic later. You might as well be dressed properly for the celebration!'

I raised an eyebrow. 'The celebration of Naqada's return to the oasis?'

She shook her head. 'No – silly! A celebration of our escape!'

Then she hurriedly stripped and washed and oiled herself and wrapped a short half tunic woven with bright coloured patterns around her waist so that her breasts remained bare. She rubbed palm oil into the wild tangles of her dark hair. It gleamed in the lamplight, and her bracelets shirred against each other as she worked. Then she hung large gold hoops from her ears and slipped a small jewelled dagger into a sheath strapped to her hips and patted her hand against it.

She shrugged and laughed as she caught my look. 'This is my dance outfit. I don't plan to cross the desert like this! And don't look so fearful, I'm not going to stab anyone either! Now, some eye-paste. And since the sun has already set, to wear paste now *is*

149

vanity! But why shouldn't we?' She laughed. 'It's a celebration!'

She dipped into a jar of grey galena paste and rubbed her thumb over my eyelids. I could smell the sweet perfume of almonds and cumin seeds on her breath as she drew around my eyes with a kohl stick.

'There! You look like a goddess! Just one more thing.' She touched the pair of cowries at her neck, then undid the leather cord and removed one shell. She held it up for me to see the underneath. 'It's from the Red Sea. Stone of the Water's Edge. The power of it comes from its eye shape. Its magic is as strong as any wedjat eye! We'll each wear one. Then we'll be sisters in spirit.'

She undid my amulet necklace and threaded the single cowrie shell alongside the eye wedjat. The two amulets lay against my neck as strange companions. One a natural eye shape, all the way from the sea on the other side of the world – the other the moonstone eye my mother had given me. They were powerful protection.

I thought of my mother's mirror still safely in my girdle bag, and drew it out and looked into it. A very different person stared back at me. With no access to a razor scalpel, my hair had grown stubby and my normally pale skin was sunburnt and dark.

Anoukhet's eyes flashed as she laughed at my surprised expression.

'We need headbands.' She reached into a leather pouch and took out some red strips. 'Tie these around your forehead. The seven red ribbons of Hathor. They'll bind her opposite fighting spirit – the Lioness, Sekhmet – and protect us tonight! And we'll wear a piece of linen fastened around the throat as well.' She laughed as she grabbed a length of material and ripped it into two strips. 'Let's wear them all. Red ribbons around our foreheads and linen around our necks. Tonight Hathor shields us! We are protected from her lioness spirit! We are *lions* ourselves!'

She flung back her wild hair so that the red ribbons swirled around her shoulders and picked up a tambourine and shook it so that the discs ruffled against each other and joined the tinkling music of the silver charms on her bracelets. Then she struck the tight parchment stretched across the hoop sharply with her fingers . . . three times. 'To sisters in spirit! To adventures ahead! To—'

'To our escape!' I said quickly, before she was able. She flashed a smile at me, then threw her arms about me and danced me around. 'To our escape!' she laughed against my ear while her monkey scampered between our feet. 'See, even Kyky is celebrating!' Then she threw back her head and romped until I was giddy and we fell laughing in a tangle on the goat-skins.

The music and lamplight and prospect of what lay ahead had set her alight and put fire to my own mood. I clutched her hand and together we strode out of the tent.

CHAPTER FOURTEEN

NAQADA

'Where have you been?' Tuthmosis demanded as we emerged. He was standing on the pathway between the braziers, his tunic filthy and his arms and legs smeared with dried mud and dust.

I shot a look at him. 'Where have *you* been?'

He flicked his hand over his body. 'Where do you think? The Medjay have enjoyed watching a king's son work. I've only just escaped. I've been tending the camels. Tethering them and feeding them and watering them. Not dressing up and tying ribbons and scarves around myself!'

He looked us up and down. 'Why are you dressed like that?'

I saw him take in Anoukhet in her dancing skirt with her bare breasts, wild hair and jewelled dagger. I wasn't sure if it was distaste or desire that I saw flicker in his eyes. Then he turned to me. 'Your outfit's not suitable.'

'Not suitable for what?' I tossed my head, so the red ribbons flew about my shoulders.

'Not suitable for anything! You're dressed too frivolously.'

I felt my jaw stiffen. 'Who are you to say what I can and cannot wear?'

'It's for your own protection, Kara. All those ribbons and the things around your neck will only draw attention. I've seen how Naqada looks at you!'

I stared back at him. 'So now you are my protector?'

He shrugged and changed the subject. 'Where have you been all this time?'

'Working as well. Baking bread.'

Anoukhet glanced at both of us in turn. 'This is no time to fight. We have to have our wits about us.'

I shot a look at Tuthmosis. 'Anoukhet has a plan for tonight.'

'Wait!' Anoukhet interrupted. 'The three of us

154

mustn't be seen together like this. They'll suspect something.'

He turned to her. 'Suspect what?'

'Sshh! Not so loud! Don't attract attention!' Then she wrinkled her nose at him and gave him a playful push. 'Go off and bathe yourself, Tuthmosis. When you're dressed and cooled off, I'll explain everything.'

Her words worked like a snake charmer's music. His anger subsided and disappeared, to be replaced with a tired smile.

She flashed a smile back at him. 'Go now. I'll look out for you later. I must speak to the camel tender.' She waved and disappeared down a path with Kyky scampering along after her.

Tuthmosis gave me a look. 'The ribbons are silly.'

'It would be sillier not to wear them! They're to tie up the scorpions of Seqet.' I turned on my heel and walked away from him. He reached out and gripped my arm tightly.

'Be careful, Kara! Don't you see? The girl's wild and will teach you wild ways. She could mean even worse trouble for us.'

'Hah! Worse trouble?' I pulled my arm free and stood glaring at him. 'What could be worse than knowing we are going to be sold back to Thebes?

Or killed here in the desert? What's worse than *that*? She can't get us into any more trouble than we're in already. She's trying to help. And if you're talking about wild ways, it's *you* who should be careful. I saw you looking at her!' I pushed past him and walked on.

'Stop being so headstrong, Kara!' he hissed after me.

Darkness settled on the camp with a sky so black, it fell like a thick, heavy cloak across my shoulders – a dark cloak spangled with more stars than a sky could surely hold.

Beyond the tents, in an open space, huge fires with flames plaiting upwards sent showers of sparks into the night. Musicians were already plucking at strings of lutes and lyres. And an old man sat tapping a tambourine. When I got closer I saw he was in fact a young man, sitting hunched and staring unseeing down at the ground. His eyelids were scarred and the sockets behind them dark, empty and hollow.

Naqada's hawk? I shuddered at the thought.

Girls sat on reed mats in the firelight, dressed in brightly striped wraps with heavy curved collars of beads about their necks, cones of perfumed wax on

156

their heads and their hair plaited and tied with mimosa blossom and small beads. Some were playing double flutes while their friends clapped and sang. Every now and again a few jumped up and did a lively dance, the huge gold discs hanging from their ears and the bracelets on their arms glinting in the firelight.

Serving girls walked bare-breasted between the people with huge reed trays resting on their shoulders, heaped with dishes of goat and fowl, steaming bowls of cracked durum wheat flavoured with dried apricots and mint, and platters of honey and figs, barley bread and goat's cheese.

Music and perfume and flavours filled the night air until my head felt giddy. I kept to myself, as did both Tuthmosis and Anoukhet, so we wouldn't be spotted together. I saw no sign of the man who had captured us – the leader, Naqada.

Much later, when the feasting had come to an end, a group of men burst into the open sandy space with flaming torches, tossing them high into the air between each other and catching them again with ease. The eyes of the crowd lost their wine-glazed look and flashed with excitement at this new entertainment. One after another the men extinguished the flames in their mouths and as they breathed out again, flags of fire burst from their throats in a sudden whoosh to the roar of the crowd's appreciation.

Then Naqada strode forward amidst cheers, his chest and arms oiled and gleaming, a sharp-bladed sickle sword clenched in one hand and with his hawk on his shoulder, attached by cord to his other wrist. He unclasped the cord and handed the bird to a fellow Medjay.

As the music grew louder and the beat livelier, he began a wild dance, swirling and twisting and brandishing his sword dangerously close to the people at the edge of the circle. I felt a whoosh of air brush my face. It was a test of skill. But also of belief in his skill. One small stumble, one slip, would have had someone's cheek sliced off, or neck cut through and one sharp, intended thrust could have found the heart of an unsuspecting opponent.

Someone grabbed my arm and pulled me back. It was Tuthmosis. He drew me deeper into the crowd, away from the slashing sword and said something I couldn't hear. But I could see by his eyes that Anoukhet had told him her plan.

Naqada was joined by a group of his fellow Medjay swordsmen. Now the music was even faster as they danced and reeled about. Pomegranates were hurled into the air and were swiftly sliced through by the swirling swords. The crowd cheered as the red seeds rained down like garnets over them.

Suddenly, someone threw up a live fowl. It squawked and beat it wings in surprise at being so high up in the air. With the swiftness of lightning finding its mark – and just as deadly – a sword swept upwards and decapitated the fowl before it could even start its downward plunge. Blood sprayed in an arc against the firelight. The crowd roared.

Despite the heat of the fires I felt myself shiver and my fingers sought Tuthmosis's hand. Across the circle I caught Anoukhet's eyes.

Another fowl was thrown up. And another and another – sliced through, decapitated, or impaled – until the air vibrated with beating wings and heads and feathers flew and blood spurted and spattered and sprayed in all directions, and the stained sand became a mess of limp, torn bodies.

A shrill, animal alarm call silenced the crowd.

In the centre of the arena one of the Medjay stood holding Kyky by the scruff of its neck. The monkey squealed and shrieked and struggled to free itself. Anoukhet screamed and rushed forward, but just as quickly her arms were grabbed by two men.

'Never! Never! Never!' she shouted as she kicked and thrashed and tried to bite their hands.

Naqada stepped into the centre space. His eyes glinted as he glanced at Anoukhet and the crowd began to chant. Then he nodded at the Medjay to throw the monkey up into the air.

I turned my head away and fought the urge to vomit. How evil could this man be? How evil were these people that they could encourage this? Wouldn't someone stop him?

I couldn't bear to watch but out of the corner of my eye I caught the blur of the small animal somersaulting upwards – its body twisting and turning in midair as it shrieked and attempted to right itself. I saw Naqada's sword flash as it shot upwards to strike on the downward fall. But at the last moment, he swept his sword arm sideways and caught hold of the monkey with his other hand and held it against his chest.

There was a glint of power in his eyes as he turned to Anoukhet. She stood slack and helpless, her arms still held by the two men. I couldn't bear to look at her face.

Then unexpectedly Naqada spun around and tossed the monkey towards me. The crowd cheered and clapped. I clutched the small, squealing bundle, not sure what to make of the moment, or what Naqada would do next. He had known *exactly* where I was standing. A shudder ran through me at the thought of him knowing – of his eyes picking me out from the crowd. Suddenly I felt weak. He had done this dreadful thing to prove something to me! *I* was his target!

Under the silvery fur, the small heart throbbed wildly against my fingers and then in one violent struggle Kyky pulled free and leaped up into the branches of a palm tree overhead. I caught Naqada's horrible smile. Then he clapped and ordered the musicians to play.

'Dance for us now, Anoukhet!' he demanded. But his eyes never left my face.

She looked at him with the loathing one might reserve for a writhing snake. Then she shrugged off the hands of her keepers and stood upright and defiant.

'Do you hear me? Dance!' he bellowed again. 'Naqada demands it!'

In silence she took one step forward. Someone tapped a tambourine tentatively. It was the blind player. A lyre was twanged and then more lyres and tambourines, flutes and drums joined in. Slowly first, then faster and faster, as if beckoning her.

She stood at the edge of the firelight, with her hands on her hips, raking her eyes over the faces around her. Then she tossed her head and began her dance – every movement exaggerated, as if she were throwing her anger at the crowd. She spun and whirled and stamped and kicked until her body was a blur. Then when the music could get no longer keep up, she threw herself forward and somersaulted over and over, faster and faster, around the circle of people.

The crowd clapped and shouted, not sensing her display was one of complete defiance and disdain for them all – but especially for Naqada.

Finally she stopped in front of him, her breath coming in gasps and sweat glistening on her skin.

I caught a quick flash of dark anticipation filling his eyes.

She stood still for a moment staring back at him. Then she drew her wrap tightly around her hips and patted the jewelled dagger and spat into the sand at his feet. For a moment I saw his hands clench and his eyes glint furiously, then he threw back his head and laughed as she turned away sharply and strode off.

CHAPTER FIFTEEN

THE SCORPION

We did as Anoukhet told us. We gathered water-skins where we could find them and goat-skins and rags of wool and found leather boots as well. After the night of celebration and drinking, the people of the oasis were not too fussed about keeping us apart, nor about where their possessions were discarded.

It was easy to find two pairs of boots that fitted and clothes that would keep us protected on the journey. Wherever we could, we stuffed our pockets and girdle bags with dates and nuts and crusts of bread. I found a whole uneaten fowl lying in a dish of spiced sauce, wrapped it in palm leaves and slipped it into a saddle bag. We were assigned no tents, so Tuthmosis and

I found some reed mats and pulled them away from the firelight to a palm tree and settled down to wait for Anoukhet to fetch us when the camp grew quiet and the time came to leave.

We whispered back and forth but soon Tuthmosis was asleep from exhaustion. I sat awake, hugging my knees to my chest, glad that we would be gone by dawn and glad that Naqada would soon be out of our lives.

But as time wore on, I began to get restless. The fires around us died down, and as the shadows closed in, so the dangers of my own thoughts seemed to close in as well. The smallest rustle above me in the palm leaves, the slightest movement of shadow, set my heart thumping. A feeling of dread came over me. Where was Anoukhet? What was taking her so long? Soon the sky would be streaked with light, and then it would be too late.

I leaned across to see if Tuthmosis was still sleeping, then got up quietly so as not to disturb him and went in search of Anoukhet. It was hard to recall which tent I'd been in that afternoon. In the moonlight the camp appeared different and the paths confusing. With the flaps down, the tents all seemed the same. My footsteps fell silently in the soft sand. Here and there dogs lay growling at one another and gnawing at bones and licking platters. From a tent nearby came heavy sounds of snoring and somewhere a baby cried but was soon shushed quiet again.

If I could find Kyky, I would find Anoukhet.

But it was the outline of Naqada's hawk that I spotted first. It sat tied to its perch outside a tent, its feathers silvered by the moonlight. From inside the tent came the sound of a muffled struggle. I stole to the side farthest away from the hawk, so the bird wouldn't alert Naqada, and strained my ears. Naqada was in there. I could hear his voice and the sound of his laugh. There was a girl's voice too – but it was muffled, as if something was being held, or had been tied, over her mouth.

It was Anoukhet. I was sure of it!

Then I heard Naqada laugh again. 'Sleep? Don't pretend you want to sleep!'

I slithered onto my stomach against the sand and edged a piece of the tent-flap slowly aside and peered into the shadowy space, waiting for my eyes to get used to the gloom. Against the bright moonlight filtering through the tent fabric, I saw the outline of Naqada. He had his back to me and was leaning over the girl, holding her down. By her wild tousled hair, and the tinkle of bracelet charms, I knew it was Anoukhet.

He had tied the neck scarf meant to ward off the terrors of Sekhmet so tightly over her mouth, she was barely able to utter a few grunts. Her wrists were bound behind her with the red ribbons. Pinned under him, she fought and twisted with her elbows and shoulders, and thrashed in vain with her legs. Now he was pressing the full weight of his body against her and was laughing with the evil brutality of a scorpion about to sting.

A blind anger rose up in me and swirled like a red sandstorm in my head until I thought I would choke. My jaw clenched. I slipped under the tent-flap.

Over Naqada's shoulder I saw Anoukhet's eyes widen as she spotted me. Then she looked away quickly, wanting to prevent him following her glance. She made small, anguished sounds and her head strained and jerked in a certain direction. It made him laugh all the more, at her helplessness. I followed the direction in which her head moved. Abandoned just beyond her reach, on some goat-skins spread on the sand, lay her jewelled dagger. Its blade was unsheathed. She had clearly tried to use it and Naqada had wrestled it from her.

I crept towards the dagger with the stealth of a lynx creeping up on its prey. Reached it and clasped. Then, with every muscle tensed, I sprang at his back in a blind rage. A sound like that of an animal came from my throat. There was no time to think of what I was doing – or know what I was planning.

I have no recall of plunging the blade into his back. I meant to stop him, that's all. To hold it at his throat, perhaps. But in my fury, as the weight of my body fell against him, I brought the dagger down. The tip must've punctured his lungs and found his heart.

He gasped and a low cry came from his mouth. His arms splayed backwards. Then he slumped down again with his cheek against the reed mat. For a moment I thought he was trying to fool us. But then I saw how completely still he lay and saw the dull eye staring unseeingly back at me.

Blood was coming from his mouth. It pooled on the reed mat. I knew it was blood, but the silvery moonlight had turned it black. It was everywhere. Spattered against the tent fabric. Running down his back. Seeping out from under him. My hands were covered with it.

Suddenly someone was at my side. I spun around, fearing the worst. But it was Tuthmosis. His face was a mask in the strange light as he tried to ease the handle of the dagger from my clenched fingers. I realised I was still clutching it and flung it from my hands, rubbing them against my tunic as if in the wiping I could wipe away all that had happened.

Tuthmosis helped me up. I felt drained of all strength. My hands hung limply at my sides and my legs went slack.

'What have I done?' I stared first at Tuthmosis and then at Anoukhet. She lay crouched with the body of Naqada still against her. I waited for someone to say something. 'I've killed him, haven't I?'

Neither spoke. Tuthmosis stooped forward and dragged Naqada aside. He slashed the bindings on Anoukhet's hands with the dagger and cut the gag on her mouth. For a moment his hand rested on her shoulder. 'Are you harmed?'

She shook her head and rubbed the marks where the linen had dug into her.

Tuthmosis nodded, then turned to me. His eyes were flinty in the moonlight and his jaw hard-set. 'You were right to kill him! He deserved it!'

I thought of the heart I had heard beat against my ear in the desert storm. I thought of it still and soundless now. And I felt myself begin to shiver.

I hugged my arms to my shoulders. I was shaking uncontrollably as we stared from one to another. The three of us were bound together now. Tuthmosis and I had witnessed Anoukhet entirely helpless at Naqada's mercy. And Tuthmosis and Anoukhet had in turn witnessed me murder a man.

These secrets and the truth of them were hard to bear. Looking from one to another, I could see we were bound as securely to each other as if we had pricked our fingers and written what we knew of one another in blood and then buried the papyrus. It was a blood bond as strong as any I'd had with Katep.

Anoukhet stood up abruptly and shrugged. And with that shrug, she appeared to put it all behind her. She gave one last look down at Naqada and kicked at his legs. 'Take his sword and his boots, Tuthmosis. They're fine leather and not worth wasting!' Then she turned to me and put her hands on my shoulders. 'You're not to blame. I would've done it, if he hadn't wrestled the dagger from me. I had planned to do it.'

I caught the fearlessness of her eyes. Then it dawned on me. I was such an innocent. Of course, she had planned this! It wasn't the first time this had happened with Naqada. How else had she commanded such a position in the camp? Her own private tent with all its luxuries? How else had she owned cowrie shells and expensive oils and linens?

It had happened before. Of *course*, it had happened before! I had been stupid and innocent and thought her innocent as well. Tonight had been planned. She had planned it with intent. I wanted to say something . . . but what was there to say?

We moved quickly then. There was no time for stopping. We gathered our things and found the old camel tender waiting with two camels, as promised. We left the glowing embers, the scavenging dogs and the upturned pots, passed below the last palm trees and galloped into the dark night with nothing but the stars reeling out overhead.

We faced the desert, with Sophet low on the horizon and Orion the hunter and the two bright pointer stars to guide us southwards towards the river. I prayed the discovery of Naqada's body would come long after dawn – long after the Medjay finally roused themselves from their wine-soaked slumbers. By that time we would be far on our journey.

CHAPTER SIXTEEN

INTO THE DESERT

We rode by the stars, in silence. Each with our own thoughts.

The old camel tender rode up front with Tuthmosis behind him, followed by Anoukhet and me in disguise – dressed as men in ragged robes and long leather boots, with woollen scarves about our faces to keep off the cold desert air. Swords hung from our waists. I had not been able to touch the jewelled dagger again. But Anoukhet had wiped it clean against her thigh and tucked it back into its sheath at her hip.

The fact that I had killed a man was trapped in my head like a buzzing fly. I couldn't shake free of it. Was it wrong to kill a man who was truly evil? I was tired . . . tired . . . tired. My head was dizzy. Every part of me ached. I leaned up against Anoukhet's back and allowed the roll of the camel's gait to lull me to sleep.

I woke with a jolt when the movement stopped. We had come to a standstill. The stars had disappeared and the sand was just beginning to gleam and change colour in the early light.

The camel tender nodded towards an outcrop of rocky cliffs, rising pale and chalky straight out of the desert. 'That's what I've been heading towards. The cliffs will provide shade and protection while we wait for Ra to carry the sun across the sky. I know this place. There are deep crevices where we can hide from the burning sun.'

'From the Medjay as well?' Tuthmosis asked.

The camel tender nodded. 'That too.'

'Scorpions of the earth! We'll fight them if they come after us!' Anoukhet spat into the sand from the height of the camel.

My own throat was parched. The sun was just beginning to rise and dust dervishes were already whirling along the horizon. High above us two dark specks floated on the warm thermal air currents. They were vultures. Perhaps an omen? I thought of the sacred Vulture Crown of Queen Tiy with its sweeping wings resting on its stand in Thebes and whispered a silent prayer to the Vulture Goddess. 'Protect us from the Medjay. Spread your wings over us.'

We headed towards the cliffs. They rose in long, fluted columns, smoothed and twisted into strange wind-torn shapes with jagged edges and holes worn by scouring sand. Between them, a gap made a natural passageway.

We turned off the passageway and went up a rocky incline that led to the top of the cliffs. The camels planted their feet obstinately and tried to turn back, starting up a cacophony of groans. Urged on by the old camel tender they eventually heaved us up, their splayed, leathery feet spreading to get a grip, braying and complaining all the way. At the top he tethered them in the shade of a rock. They settled on their knees and were silent at last while he began unpacking the saddlebags.

Anoukhet fiddled with something under her cloak and tipped some water from a goat-skin into her hand. A pair of small, troubled eyes peeped out from a fold in the cloak.

Tuthmosis gave her a sharp look. 'You can't have brought it!' He pulled her cloak aside.

173

Kyky sat clinging to Anoukhet like a tiny silvery-furred baby with a dark, surprised face.

'How can we travel with a monkey? You should've left it behind!'

Anoukhet glared at him. 'What? Left her behind to have her eyes gouged out by Naqada's hawk? Or have her body impaled in a fit of frenzied swordplay? Never!'

'A monkey needs feeding and watering!'

'So?'

'There are limited supplies.'

She gave a shrug, lifting one shoulder and the side of her mouth, as if there was nothing to be done about it. 'I'll give up some of my share!' Then she turned and sat, petting and stroking Kyky's head as she stared out across the desert.

Tuthmosis glared at her back, then finally sighed and turned away.

I walked to the edge of the precipice and looked out at the vast sea of sand, stretching in all directions.

'Stand back from there, Isikara!' Tuthmosis commanded.

I gave him a look and returned to where they were sitting, almost invisible in a dark patch of shade. The crevices were so deep that in contrast to the chalky rock the shadow seemed purple.

We took small sips from the goat-skin water-bag and ate the scraps of chicken I had brought along in silence. I felt Tuthmosis's eyes on me and glanced towards him from time to time. But he wouldn't meet my eye. He seemed angry and restless. What was he thinking? That I was a girl who had killed a man? So much had happened since the night alongside the river. It was hard to imagine he had ever kissed me.

I glanced across at Anoukhet. She was silent and seemed oblivious of us and not bothered by anything. She tore delicately at the chicken bones with sharp white teeth, like a gazelle nibbling the leaves from a bush. When she'd finished, she held out her fingers for Kyky to lick then wiped her hands on her robe.

Suddenly the camel tender lifted his head as if he'd caught a glimpse of something out the corner of his eye. He cupped his hands to the side of his face and focused far into the distance. I glanced at where he was looking. There seemed to be nothing but heat wavering across the sand.

'What? What can you see?'

'They're coming.'

'The Medjay?'

He nodded. 'They're following.'

Tuthmosis stood up to look. The camel tender pulled him down quickly. 'Don't break the silhouette. Keep hidden in the shadow. The Medjay have very good eyesight!'

I strained my eyes. All I saw were ribbons of swirling heat vapour, writhing and floating and dissolving far in the distance.

I glanced back at him. 'Are you sure?'

He looked at me with his toothless smile. 'I've not lived all my life in the desert for nothing. My eyes see what they see. There are five men. All of them Medjay.'

'Five?'

He nodded.

Tuthmosis looked at him impatiently. 'How do you know they're Medjay?'

'By the glint of their swords.'

'Scorpions!' Anoukhet hissed.

I stared into the distance. I could hardly make out the outlines – let alone the glint of swords. They were just shapes swirling and writhing across the horizon like trails of bleached cloth. There was no substance to them. No feet seemed to anchor them to the ground.

176

They simply floated closer and closer, dissolving and reappearing like apparitions in a dream. A feeling of dread came over me. Even in the bone dry air I felt sweat begin to prickle and break out on my skin. I dared not close my eyes as I watched the shapes forming and reforming. 'What will we do?' I whispered. 'Can we outrun them?'

'Hah!' Anoukhet's dark eyes flashed at me from the shadows. 'And let them see we're cowards? No! We'll fight them. We have our swords and daggers.'

Tuthmosis shook his head. 'We can't fight them. They outnumber us. And if we made a dash for it, we'd never outrun them. With only one man to a camel, they will be much faster than us.'

'We must neither fight nor run.'

We all turned to look at the camel tender. 'Then what?' I asked.

He grinned with a canny look to his eyes. 'I know the Medjay. I know how their minds work. They'll be in a hurry. In the mood for revenge. For an opportunity to slaughter. We have to outwit them.'

A shiver ran through me. *Slaughter!* It was such a horrible word. Visions of decapitation and sword slashes across the chest, bone crunching and blood spurting everywhere, came to me. I felt the hot stickiness of the word. The butchery of it. The blood seeping from it.

'How'll we outwit them?' Tuthmosis asked.

'By staying exactly where we are – hidden in this crevice high up in the shadow. We have the advantage. They have the sun blazing into their eyes and won't pick us up in the shade. They'll pass below through the passageway looking straight ahead, beating their camels in their hurry to catch up with us. They won't think we've stopped. They'll believe we're on the run. Heading straight towards the river, by the quickest route.'

Tuthmosis seemed unsure. 'It's quite a chance.'

The camel tender nodded. 'Our *only* chance!'

Anoukhet shook her head as if we were all mad. 'We must face them and fight it out.'

I glanced at her. She was brave enough to do just this. Wearing her tattered cloak and shredded head-band and long leather boots, she seemed as much a warrior as the Medjay themselves. But I knew I wasn't brave enough!

I turned to the old camel tender. 'What about our tracks? They'll see we've branched off and climbed up here.'

'What tracks? Look down at the sand below.' He

178

pointed to the passageway. 'The wind has already smoothed them away and the rocks show nothing of the camels' footprints.' He shook his head. 'No. They're not following our tracks. They've come this way because it's the quickest way to the Great River.'

He was right. There was no sign of where our camels had walked and nothing to suggest where we'd climbed.

Anoukhet clicked her tongue impatiently. 'We're cornered here in this crevice. Let's face them in the open.'

I looked at the camel tender. 'What if a camel brays just as they are passing? Can we tie up their jaws?'

He laughed and shook his head. 'Camels like to chew. If you tie their jaws, they make even more noise. No. We want them to be still. I'll tether them tight and . . .' he drew a leather pouch from the folds of his clothes and reached inside it, 'I'll give them these.'

'What?'

'Dates. I keep them as a treat. They love nothing better than the sweet stickiness to chew on. It'll keep them quiet. Now, get ready. Whatever you do, don't stand up. Don't break the silhouette. Stay in the shadow!'

'Hah!' hissed Anoukhet with exasperation. She

began gathering her things together and wrapped Kyky in a bundle of cloth and handed her to me. I held her tight, not sure of why I was being asked to look after her.

The Medjay were closer now. The camel tender was right. There were five of them. All heavily armed. They raced towards us with their cloaks flying out behind them. The sharpness of their shadows against the clear light carved them in my eye. In the vast empty space where nothing else was moving, they appeared even more menacing. They were coming after me. *I* was the one who had killed Naqada!

My heart thumped in my ears. It was difficult to know if it was truly my heart or the drumbeats of the camels. They were so close now, I could see the foamy spittle flying from the camels' mouths and nostrils and hear the men grunting.

As they entered the passageway, there was a movement at my side. It was Anoukhet. She was crouched like a leopard ready to leap – the dagger in her hand – waiting for the moment when they would pass exactly below us.

I tugged frantically at her arm. But she shook me off without a glance. Suddenly, there was a blur of movement. I expected to see Anoukhet flying through the air. But it was Tuthmosis who had flung himself at her. With a dull thud he wrestled her down to the ground, clamped a hand tightly across her mouth, and pinned her with the weight of his body. Then he tried to wrench the dagger from her, while she thrashed and rolled and kicked and struggled beneath him. They were still in the shadow but dangerously close to the edge. In panic I let go of the monkey and grabbed hold of Anoukhet's boots and clung to her legs.

Then I glanced down over the edge. The moment had passed. The men were through the passageway and galloping away from us, without so much as a backward glance. The noise of their camels had masked the sounds of our struggle. My heart seemed stuck somewhere. I could hardly draw breath.

'Yeow!' Tuthmosis let out a sharp curse as Anoukhet kicked violently and twisted out from under him. There was blood dripping from his hand and also on Anoukhet's lips.

She leaned panting up against a rock and glared back at us, her breath coming in gasps, her hair all tangled and her eyes dangerously glinting, blood on her teeth and mouth. More wild animal than girl.

'Cowards! All of you! It would've been better to die

181

than to do nothing!' At the sound of her voice, Kyky leaped across to her shoulder. Anoukhet spat into the sand and hissed. 'Curse you, Tuthmosis! Why did you stop me? I could've killed them all. I would've surprised them! Killed the first one I landed on. Then taken on the other four easily.'

'You could never take on four men . . .' I began to say, but was silenced by her withering glance.

'You haven't seen me! I'm deadly accurate with a throwing dagger. And my sword would have finished off the other three!'

I stared back at her. Yes. Now, with her wild animal face, I could believe she might have finished them all off!

'I had it planned,' she hissed between her bloodied teeth. 'How dare you, Tuthmosis! How dare you stop me! You think because you're the son of a king, you should be obeyed. I'm not one of your slaves. I will *not* obey you! Don't *ever* do that to me again!'

Tuthmosis stood with his hands stiffly at his sides and glared down at her. 'Don't ever *bite* me again!' was all he said.

I looked between the two of them as they stared at each other with blazing eyes, waiting to see who would turn away first. When neither did, I stepped between them without looking at either, and took Tuthmosis's hand. 'Let me rinse this and bind it for you, before you lose too much blood.'

The three of us were tied by bonds, but this was still going to be a difficult journey.

CHAPTER SEVENTEEN

ABU ISLAND

When I had finished binding Tuthmosis's hand with strips of torn linen, he nodded towards Anoukhet. 'Cut her hair! She has to look like a boy.'

'Don't you dare!' she hissed at me.

'Yours can be left, Isikara. It's short enough. But cut hers.'

I eyed him. 'Stop giving orders! Besides, there's no moss to wet it and make a lather. It can wait until we reach the river.'

'No! Cut it now, before we meet up with anyone else.'

I drew my blade reluctantly from my belt.

Anoukhet sat in silence. Then she jumped up. 'I'll

do it myself!' She snatched up her dagger – the
jewelled one that had cut to the heart of Naqada –
grabbed a fistful of her hair and hacked it off with
one quick movement. She flung the hair down and
hacked again and again.

The long black tendrils fell against the sand in
shapes as intricate and intertwined as strange hieroglyphs. It was as if they were telling their own secret
story. Something of who Anoukhet really was.

A new person stood before us, wild-eyed and shorn.
I glanced at her face but she wouldn't meet my eye.
I gathered up the thick strands and shook them free
of sand. How long had they taken to grow to such
a length? I lay the strands in a roll of cloth, bound
them up and handed them to her.

She shrugged her shoulders and tossed the bundle
into her saddlebag. I could see the glitter of tears in
her eyes. I knew they were not tears of regret, but of
anger that she had been forced to obey Tuthmosis.

Our camel was a bony and supercilious beast with
bloodshot eyes. You know a camel hates you from the
moment you first walk around him, wondering where
and how to climb up. Ours moaned and spat and
snarled as we approached it lying in the shadow.

The only way to mount a camel without help is

to get on while it's lying down and then get it to rise with you already sitting. We heaved ourselves on and sat astride with Anoukhet up front. She prodded and urged it up. In the standing-up process, we were thrown backwards and forwards twice. The four distinct jolts were each more violent and unexpected than the other. I knew the tricks of this camel. Once we were up, if we moved in the saddle, he snarled and tried to snap at us. And if Anoukhet tried to urge him in another direction, he turned to bite our feet.

But she seemed not the least bit bothered by any of this as she forced the camel forward down the cliff path.

After a long silent afternoon of neverending sand dunes, endlessly rippling towards the horizon, I sensed the camels' sudden change of pace and knew we must be nearing the river. Suddenly we came over a rise of amber sand-slopes and found ourselves looking down on a landscape of black boulders, tumbled and glistening in the sun like polished jet.

The Great River lay before us – but different to any part of the river I'd seen so far. Instead of smooth-flowing water with banks of sand and mud, the river was choppy and white-curdled as it rushed and tumbled over, around and between the huge, smooth black rocks.

Upstream to my left was a green island, so large it seemed almost like the opposite bank, except I could see water flowing around its tip, dividing the river into two channels. It could only be the fabled island of Abu – Elephant Island, named after its huge boulders that looked like the backs of elephants, wallowing in the water.

It was rugged and high to the south with the stone walls of a temple rising up in the distance and a coastline of creeks, small sandy beaches and groves of palm and mimosa and castor oil shrubs coming down to the water's edge. There were tilled patches of cotton plants, lentils and durra, and wild flowers, making the green heart of the island.

After the harshness of the desert, it was like a beautiful jewel set in the river. I let out a long sigh. 'We're safe at last!

Tuthmosis shook his head. 'Not yet! We aren't beyond the control of Thebes yet. My father built that temple and a harbour for his army. There'll be Egyptian soldiers here. We must travel further south still.'

My heart sank.

Anoukhet shook her head. 'We can't move on directly. We need to cross to Syene first.' She indicated the opposite bank of the river and a sprawl of mud-brick houses with dark-mouthed alleyways between them. 'There'll be food and a chance to rest.'

'And soldiers as well! No! It's too dangerous. They'll be on the lookout for us.'

Anoukhet laughed as she gave him a swift glance. 'Not looking like this! You hardly look like a Royal Prince! Besides, there's no settlement further south beyond these cataracts, not for a long while. There'll be no marketplace or chance of food again. And I know my way around Syene.'

We urged the camels onto a barge that took us to the other side. The bank was crowded with people and bales of goods, with heaps of dates spilling out of woven baskets and donkeys and camels both laden and unladen. Rotting, half-sunk boats lay poking out of the mud and dried-out hulls lay between the reeds in the afternoon sunshine. The edge of the river itself was covered with boats moored so tightly together that they made a solid raft over which people crossed and recrossed as they loaded and unloaded goods. Beyond them men paddled from shore to shore in small reed boats, dragging fishing nets.

Above the sound of the cataracts, came the noise of barking dogs, shrill voices, camels snorting and snarling, donkeys braying and the clamour of dealers shouting and children squealing and splashing.

As we rode between them they held their goods at arm's length, begging us to stop and look and buy. What was offered seemed new and strange compared to what we'd seen in markets before. Ostrich eggs, claws, teeth, spears, bows, arrows, ebony clubs and daggers; strange wrinkled animal hides, whips of hippopotamus hide, leather girdles decorated with glass beads and cowrie shells, human skulls – or so they looked – and sloughed snake skins.

Down narrow alleyways, powerful and exciting aromas came from mounds of red, gold and brown powders, curious-looking roots, shrivelled pods and strange bulbs and young boys ran alongside us offering handfuls. Anoukhet was leaning down from the camel, laughing and arguing, seeming delighted to touch and feel and smell everything that was thrust towards us. When a boy handed her a flask of castor oil she pulled out the stopper and held it to her nose then immediately began rubbing her arms with the strong-smelling unguent. Then she laughed and handed him her strip of goat's wool scarf in exchange.

'Stop that!' Tuthmosis hissed. 'You're behaving like a girl!'

Anoukhet raised an eyebrow. 'Boys use perfume too. Didn't you ever rub oil into your skin when you lived in the Palace?'

'Shssh! Don't speak of the Palace! You'll get us caught!'

She flashed a look at him. 'This is my place! I know how to behave here! It's *you* who is the stranger. You forget I'm Nubian. I'm named after the Goddess of all Nubia – Anoukhet – Goddess of the Hunt! Goddess of the Waters of the Great River! This is my *home*.'

'I need to find my people!' the old camel tender announced, looking between the two of them. 'You've no more need of me. I brought you safely through the desert, now I must leave you.' He nodded towards Anoukhet. 'Keep your camel. I'll take this one in payment.'

We bade him farewell and Tuthmosis slid down and untied his saddlebag. It seemed to amuse Anoukhet that we rode while he walked alongside us.

He caught her look. 'We'll be selling that camel soon. We'll need to buy a boat to go further downstream.'

Anoukhet shook her head. 'Have you seen the

cataracts? Boats aren't used to travel downstream on this part of the river. It's too wild. Camels and donkeys transport everything along the banks around the cataracts.' She nodded her head towards one of the shadowy, dark alleyways. 'There's a place down there to get food and drink.'

Tuthmosis shook his head. 'It looks rough. There might be soldiers from the garrison.'

Anoukhet flashed a look at him and laughed as she made the camel kneel, dismounted then tied it to a post. 'So? We're not girls, remember! I'm thirsty and hungry. Come on,' she urged. 'Let's not argue about this.'

She removed Kyky from under her wrap and placed her on her shoulder. Tuthmosis glared after her as she marched down the alleyway. 'You'll only bring attention with that animal.'

'There'll be more than monkeys in here to attract attention,' she said as she ducked through the doorway.

CHAPTER EIGHTEEN

ENCOUNTERS

The rowdiness and noise of the room hit me as we entered. It was full of soldiers. They were a rough-looking bunch, dishevelled and unshaven. Serving girls moved swiftly between them, carrying trays of sweetmeats and palm wine. When my eyes got used to the gloom, I noticed there were other girls as well, dressed flamboyantly in bright wraps, their breasts bare and their hairstyles elaborate, with swathes of beads around their necks and large gold trinkets swinging from their ears. They laughed and moved about among the men, pouting and taking sips of wine and sitting on their laps.

Tuthmosis pulled at my arm. 'It's nothing but a

whoring house. We can't stay! We'll find food and drink in the marketplace.'

Anoukhet laughed up at him. 'Are you scared of these women? It's just a bit of fun. We've been cut off from merriment for too long in the desert.'

As Tuthmosis turned to walk out, I touched his arm. 'We can't split up now. We're travelled so far together. We won't stay long. We'll have some-thing to eat and drink and then we'll be off.' I glanced across at Anoukhet but she was already seated with a girl, who was stroking the monkey and tickling her neck.

'What's its name?'

'Kyky,' Anoukhet replied.

'And your name, my sweet?' The girl stroked Anoukhet's face and cupped her hands under her chin so that she could look at her. 'What a handsome boy you are with skin as smooth as a baby's, not a sign of a beard and perfumed so sweetly with castor oil!' She tucked her arms around Anoukhet's waist, slipped onto her lap and whispered something in her ear.

Tuthmosis tugged at my arm. 'This is sickening. Come! We must leave!'

But at that moment two girls sidled up on either

side of us. One draped her arm about my neck. 'Do your mothers know you sweet boys are here?'

I could sense the blood rising to my cheeks and could not bring myself to even glance at Tuthmosis.

'What innocence! He's blushing!'

I felt a hand run against my leg and pulled away. 'I'm . . .' I couldn't think what to say. 'We're hungry and thirsty! We've ridden through the desert.'

'Straight from the desert! But *you're* not Medjay! Not with your foreign accents and fine manners. And not with those beautiful blue eyes of his!' She nodded her head at Tuthmosis.

Damn! He had forgotten to pull his head-dress down over his eyes!

The woman clicked her fingers at a serving girl. 'Bring some wine and sweetbreads for these poor fine boys, before they faint.'

I smiled and nodded. 'Yes . . . we are hungry.'

She laughed. 'I know . . . and you smell like a camel. But I'll soon have you bathed and clean.'

I turned to Tuthmosis in confusion, imagining she would lead me off at any moment. I could feel the blood burning in my face.

'No! I don't need to bathe!'

'*You* might believe you don't – but I know better.'

Tuthmosis rested a firm hand on the woman's shoulder. 'I think my friend is exhausted. It's more food than a bath that he needs.'

She smiled at me. 'Of course. A drink first.' She led me to a bench, pushed me down and sat on my lap. 'Here!' she held a cup to my lips. 'Drink.'

The palm wine ran down my throat like fire. I choked and spluttered. 'I need water!'

'Poor baby! Too young for palm wine. Is this your first time in a place like this?'

I nodded. 'Don't be scared then.' She ran her hands over her body, smiling enticingly. 'Here, give me your hands.'

But before she could take hold of them, I snatched them away and sat on them.

She tousled my head. 'Poor boy! Don't be so shy!'

'Could I please have some water and food?' I stammered.

She reached for a sweetmeat, brought her face up close to mine and fed it to me between my lips. I tried to back away but I was against a wall. Just when I thought she would kiss me, Tuthmosis pushed her roughly aside. 'Leave the boy alone!'

The girl scrambled up. She looked at us with flashing eyes. 'I see! You're jealous! Is *that* how it is

between the two of you then? You don't like women?'
Then she turned to me. 'Well, there's no place for the
likes of you two pretty boys *here*, then. Coming in
here and leading a girl on!' she hissed as she slapped
me hard on the face.

Tuthmosis grabbed hold of her arm. 'I said, leave
him be! He's my younger *brother*!'

'Hah! I've heard that one before!' She took a long
look at Tuthmosis and would have slapped him as
well except he still held her.

'Scum . . . that's what you are! Nothing but scum!
What right have you to come in here in your smelly,
filthy clothes and put on airs and graces far above
yourself, when you go after boys!' And with the arm
that was free, she swung back and punched him hard
in the stomach. It was so unexpected that Tuthmosis
crumpled forward.

A group of soldiers had gathered about us –
dishevelled, sunburnt men with bloodshot eyes, but
well-muscled, wearing rough wraps and gold armbands
with sickle swords in their belts. I could see they were
foot soldiers of the Egyptian army – hardy infantry-
men used to sleeping out in the open on rough terrain
and to protecting themselves in all situations. They
formed a circle and eyed us as the room fell silent.

One, who stood a head taller than Tuthmosis, narrowed his eyes and turned to the girl. 'Is he giving you trouble, Maya?' Without waiting for an answer he took a swipe at Tuthmosis's head with his fist that left a bloody gash at the side of his temple. As Tuthmosis fell, the soldier swung back his boot and kicked him hard in the stomach.

'Stop!' But before I could do anything, I felt Anoukhet at my side.

'Let's go!' she hissed.

Between us, we dragged Tuthmosis upright and shouldered him towards the entrance, with Kyky jumping up and down and shrieking in agitation and the sneers and curses of the women as well as the soldiers at our backs.

We crept into a secluded side-alley next to the marketplace. I held Tuthmosis's head in my lap while Anoukhet went to fetch water from the river. He lay without moving as he had so long ago in the labyrinth. Except that now it was entirely *my* fault he was unconscious. He had been protecting me.

Anoukhet returned, wrung out a cloth in the water she carried in her goat-skin and laid it across his forehead, while I bathed the blood from the wound.

'They might come after us, don't you think?' I said.

'I doubt it.'

'Why not?

'I gave the girl I was with a gift. She said she'd help us.'

'What sort of gift?'

She shrugged. 'No matter. I settled it with her. She'll protect us and see we're not followed. She'll distract them. She promised.'

I squinted back at her. 'What do you mean, settled it? What did you do? Did you . . .?' I felt my breath catch and looked up at her sharply.

'Silly! I gave her my hair.'

'Your hair? Why?'

'To make a wig. Besides . . . she discovered I was a girl.'

I eyed Anoukhet's face. 'How?'

'She felt my breasts.'

'How could you let her do that?'

'Don't be so innocent! She kissed me, of course!

'Kissed you – another girl?'

'What's a kiss? She thought I was a boy. So I let her. But when I saw there was going to be trouble with the soldiers, I made her promise not to tell we were girls and gave her my hair. So we're safe from them. They won't come after us.'

At last I found my voice. 'She took more than your hair.'

'What do you mean?'

'Your silver bracelet with the animal charms has gone.'

For a moment Anoukhet looked startled as she glanced down at her wrist. But then she made light of it and shrugged. 'No matter! If I'm to be a boy, it's better I don't wear trinkets. But as soon as Tuthmosis recovers, we must move on.'

'Do you think his wounds are serious?'

'There's more blood than true damage. The cut's not deep but he'll have a black eye. The soldiers will recognise us now. We must leave Syene as soon as possible.'

'Aren't you going to search for your family?'

'They could be dead for all I know. Taken into slavery. Sold or made to work in the quarries, cutting stone for obelisks and statues for Thebes. There's no reason for me to stay.' She gave a broad smile. 'Besides, you're my family now. You and Tuthmosis.'

'You fight with him all the time.'

'Don't brothers and sisters always fight? You don't . . . because you're not a sister to him.'

'What am I then?'

'You're an innocent – that's what you are, if you don't already know!'

'Know what?'

'He's in love with you.'

'Don't be silly! He's not!' I glanced down quickly to see if Tuthmosis was awake and felt myself blushing. 'Besides, he's a king. Kings can't be in love with the daughters of priests. And there's someone else he loves, anyway.'

'If he's not in love with you, why did he try to prevent that girl from kissing you?'

I felt my cheeks get redder at the thought of it.

Anoukhet shook her head. 'No. I saw it all. He's in love with you.'

CHAPTER NINETEEN

SERPENT OF THE DESERT

We slept in a doorway that night, huddled together between the debris of broken pieces of pottery, mud bricks and chicken bones with Kyky nestling between us and jumping up and screeching every time a dog came sniffling or a rat ran by.

The market noises woke us long before dawn. Tuthmosis stirred, groaned and held his head, complaining of a terrible headache. I was embarrassed to catch his eye after what Anoukhet had announced. To avoid facing him I went down to the river to fetch water to bathe his wounds.

The market was busy and noisy even though it was not properly light. Under an awning strung with lanterns, skin merchants were scraping fresh hides, cutting them and stretching them over frames to make into shields. Ironmongers, already black and sweaty, were casting molten liquids into moulds around their fires. An array of spearheads and arrowheads lay in the sand and the air was filled with the hollow chime of the rough iron edges being tapped off against anvils. Girls were setting out cucumbers and pomegranates and newly-baked cakes onto mats on the ground. Between them were jars of goats' milk covered by pieces of goat-skin, still shaggy with hair.

As I approached the river I saw some Egyptian foot soldiers encamped at the water's edge. I scrutinised their faces to see if I recognised any of them. It was hard to tell. Going about their ordinary tasks, they were very different to the brutes of the night before. Some were seated on the ground, having their heads shaved. Others were sharpening swords while a man sweeping the ground next to them was being supervised to sprinkle water to settle the dust.

The smell of bread baking and the aroma of sizzling meat coming from the alleyways made me hungry. But I knew it was unsafe to linger and pulled my cloak about me, scooped water and left as soon as I could.

'The camel's gone.' Anoukhet announced as soon as I reached the doorway.

'Gone?'

'Stolen. One of us should've stayed awake to keep watch.' She took the water-skin and began swabbing Tuthmosis's face.

'You hated that miserable camel anyhow!' Tuthmosis squinted up at me through swollen eyes. With his hand still bandaged from Anoukhet's bite and his face bruised and battered, he looked so odd that for a moment I forgot what Anoukhet had told me the night before and smiled. He attempted to smile in return but ended up grimacing with pain.

'We'll need donkeys to get beyond the cataracts,' Anoukhet said as she dabbed at his face. She seemed to be trying to make amends with Tuthmosis. 'We'll hire ourselves out to load goods that have to be transported upstream. No one will think to look for the Prince of Thebes on a donkey!'

A hubbub of shouts coming from the marketplace and a fearful drumming of boots against stone as soldiers marched by the end of our alleyway silenced us. Each man carried a copper-bladed spear and shield and in their belts were axes and swords.

'What's happening?' Anoukhet asked a passer-by.

'Some Medjay rode in from the desert last night and told of three felons who stole two camels and escaped their camp after murdering their leader!' He spat in the sand. 'That's no loss! But there's whispered one of the felons is none other than Prince Tuthmosis, son of King Amenhotep.'

'What?' Anoukhet could not resist. 'I thought he'd died and his brother ruled in his place.'

The man shook his head. 'It's said not. There's a rumour of skulduggery.'

'What sort of skulduggery?'

The man drew a wedjat eye in the dust and looked over his shoulder. Then he came closer and whispered. 'No one knows the truth – Syene being so far from Thebes. The news we get by boat is muddled. But they say there was a plot afoot to have him murdered.'

'To have who murdered?'

'Prince Tuthmosis. It's said he didn't die of natural causes. It's said the High Priests of Thebes were involved in the plot. That they preferred the younger brother so they could mould him to their wishes.'

Tuthmosis shrugged and pulled at his headscarf. 'You can't believe rumours.' But after the man left us,

204

he jumped up. 'We can't stay a moment longer. It's not safe. We have to move quickly.'

Down at the river we began negotiating with the donkey men.

They looked askance at us and laughed. 'What? The three of *you*? We need strong-muscled men to shift the weight of the loads, not *boys*!'

Each one we approached had something disparaging to say about Anoukhet's and my slight builds. And they laughed directly at Tuthmosis when they saw his face. 'Two black eyes! Been in a brawl, have you? We need tough workers here, not boys who can so easily be knocked about. And not one with a limp like yours, either!'

I saw Tuthmosis's face drain and his fists clench. I thought he might lash out, so I tugged his arm and urged him on. His misfortune was, in truth, our good luck, as his two black eyes hid the blue of his irises and made him less recognisable.

Kyky ran ahead, chasing lizards that basked on the rocks in the sun, and scampering across the boats, snatching up beetles that scuttled out of plaited mats and from sacks being unpacked.

A man loading up his donkeys stopped to laugh at her.

'Have you any work?' Anoukhet asked.

He eyed us and shook his head. 'Come back when you've grown a little.'

'I'm strong!' Anoukhet flung her cloak aside and showed the strength of her bare arms. It was true – rubbed with castor oil and gleaming in the sunshine, her shoulders looked very powerful.

The donkey man tossed his head and laughed delightedly. 'A beautiful body! If you were a girl, I'd invite you to be my wife! But you're a boy – and not strong enough to load and unload donkeys all day long!' He bent down to pick up a huge sack as if to demonstrate his own bulging strength.

Suddenly Kyky screeched. Anoukhet spun around, clutching her dagger and threw it. My heart stopped at the sound of it flying past my face. I expected the man to fall dead at our feet with the dagger straight through his heart.

But instead he jumped aside. Only then did I see what had happened. Lying right at his feet was a terrible-looking snake – long and scaly, with two horns that stood up behind its vicious eyes. It stared at us through narrow, black, vertical pupil slits, while a thin, dark tongue flicked.

I leaped back as it suddenly flung its coils forward.

But the snake was impaled. Anoukhet's dagger had pinned it firmly just below the base of its skull to the hard clay of the riverbank. It twisted and thrashed uselessly.

The man was too shocked to speak.

'A horned viper – one of the most poisonous snakes in all Egypt and Nubia!' Anoukhet hissed as she snatched up the dagger from the flesh of the snake and in one swift stroke – too fast to follow – sliced through its neck. So fast, that the snake scarcely had time to recoil its body before its head lay separate on the ground, with the rest of its coils still writhing.

I gaped at her then found my voice. 'That was foolish! It could have struck you!'

She flicked the head aside and gave me a scornful look. 'I know horned vipers. I've come across plenty in the desert. They lie in ambush, waiting for their prey under a rock, or side-winding and digging into the sand so only their horns show.'

Her words echoed a warning in my ears.

They bury themselves in the sands of the desert and shelter under rocks, waiting to do evil. Fast, unpredictable, poisonous! They're the most dangerous inhabitants of this earth. Serpents of the Underworld.

Anoukhet had been speaking of Naqada then. The same dagger that killed the snake had killed him.

I thought of the rearing cobra on Tuthmosis's father's forehead in the tomb and shuddered. Tuthmosis's brother was wearing the cobra now. The viper had been a warning. Naqada was dead but the rearing cobra would still come after us.

The threat of Wosret would never leave us.

In Amenhotep's burial chamber, the flared cobras dangling dangerously at Hathor's ears had been for protection. I prayed for her protection now. Hathor – Protector of Women. Goddess of the Moon.

I watched Anoukhet cut a thin, precise line down the belly of the viper and ease the flesh away from the skin with the tip of her forefinger. Her hands worked quickly and accurately.

The man found his voice. 'You struck so fast. Like a bolt of lightning! How did you know the viper was behind me, hiding under the rock?'

'Kyky warned me. Then I heard the scraping sound of its scales before I saw it. A viper rasps them together as it coils back, before it strikes. Usually it only hunts lizards but you disturbed it when you crouched next to the rock.'

'Praise Horus! I'll take you on. We need someone who's fast with a dagger. There are thieves and felons here alongside the cataracts. There's been a murder, they say, and three felons are in Syene, ready to do murder again. Anyone as skilled as you are with a dagger will be good to have with us on the donkey trail.'

'No felons will get the better of me!' She threw the piece of snake flesh to some dogs that began to scrap over it immediately and nodded towards us. 'And them? What about them? Will you take them on as well?'

The man eyed us, then shrugged. 'There'll be no pay except food.'

Anoukhet stood up and wiped the blood off her hands. She meticulously rolled the viper skin into a coil and placed it in her saddlebag. Then she met his eye with a casual glance but I saw the curve at the corner of her lips. 'That's enough for us!'

'Well, get to it fast then, and load the donkeys. We need to leave before the day gets too hot. But first, eat some food for strength.' He handed us a loaf of bread, an urn of buttermilk and a handful of dates. Then he nodded at Anoukhet. 'You did well!'

The buttermilk slipped down my throat as sweet as honey. Yes . . . perhaps it *was* Hathor who had sent Anoukhet to us.

The bags of grain were heavier than I imagined and the donkeys we loaded them onto seemed too small for the weight of them. But the boat was eventually unloaded and empty and ready to be hauled down the river by Nubian slaves.

We had already climbed on the donkeys in front of our loads, when we were stopped by two Egyptian soldiers. For a moment, as they eyed us, I thought they might order us down. Tuthmosis had pulled his headscarf around his face. It hid his swollen black eyes. I prayed Anoukhet would be silent.

The donkey owner spoke up. 'They're just boys, helping me transport this load across the cataracts. I hired them not for their muscle but their cheapness.'

The soldiers nodded and passed on to the next group. I caught Tuthmosis's relieved look and smiled back at him.

We were joined by a few more teams of donkey men who took up the trail behind us.

It was too hot to hurry the donkeys. A dry wind had sprung up and blew the dust around us in eddies and flies buzzed about our faces, drawn by the sweat of the donkeys. Along the rocky path were the whitened bones of some poor creature. Perhaps an ailing donkey that had been too tired to step any further. We trudged up a rise alongside the river, and from here I got my first view of the landscape of Nubia.

Under a white sky, hazy with heat, it had a brassy appearance. Confused jagged peaks and twisted ravines of cliffs seemed like metal cast and beaten by the sun. In front of us a golden-yellow plateau of sand lay dazzling in the sunshine. Beyond this, paths of sand wound between the ravines and the confusion of black rocks and savage-toothed hills.

Away and away it stretched, ending somewhere in the far distance in a purple blur. Like a place of utter despair – once entered, never returned from.

Eventually we lost sight of the river and came to a hard, flattened landscape where we rested under some scraggy thorn trees. Later, when the sun had set, we came across a group of traders. As we got nearer, we heard their music and singing, coming to us through the green evening light. A meal was being prepared and around the fires were groups of men and a few grunting camels and donkeys and shaggy black goats. We offloaded our donkeys and sat to one side of their circle, preparing our own meal.

A man sat tapping lightly against a hide-covered tambourine that made soft jingling sounds and sang in a quiet, plaintive voice. A boy played a reed pipe alongside him. I watched Anoukhet stroll across to them. I thought she might begin to dance but instead she sat down wordlessly in the sand, picked up another flute, put it to her lips and began to play.

The thin reed music quavered through the air and the man's voice rose and fell in trembling sounds that seemed to come not from his throat, but from somewhere deep inside him, filling the night with unknown longing.

I looked across at Tuthmosis and wondered what he was thinking. Suddenly I knew I had to chase away the sadness. I reached into my girdle bag and drew out my father's Senet box.

'Will you teach me the game?'

We laid out the pieces on the board and settled down in the sand that still held the warmth of the sun and played until the coals burned down and the night turned grape-blue at our backs.

CHAPTER TWENTY

THE BELLY OF STONES

By the time we reached the second cataract, with the forts of Semna and Kumma facing each across the Belly of Stones, we had been travelling with the donkey men, southwards along the Great River, for more than a moon and had already passed the forts of Buhen and Askut which protected the furthermost reaches of Egypt.

The donkey owner from Syene was impressed by our diligence. But our attention to his commands was merely to avoid the attention of others. To dodge the eye of the Egyptian garrisons, we volunteered extra duties that kept us out of sight. The donkey men thought us too shy to join them when they went off drinking in the markets, but our experience in Syene had taught us to be careful.

'We can't travel endlessly with the donkey men,' Anoukhet said one afternoon as we sat on some rocks beneath a straggly mimosa tree near the cataracts. She was playing my favourite game – flinging out flat pebbles to see how far they would skip.

I shook my head. 'You won't manage here. They won't jump. The water's too rough!'

Below us the river swept past, dashing and throwing itself from rocky ledge to rocky ledge, between islands of strange, water-worn shapes. I narrowed my eyes and looked into the glare.

Some boys were shouting and playing downstream. They had thrown off their wraps and were shooting the rapids, sitting astride pieces of wood and clinging on as the force of the water tossed them up through the foaming torrent, then disappearing again as the waves dashed them wildly along. One boy came down a slope of water, riding it on his stomach, his arms fighting the river like the spokes of a wheel – to the wild cheers of the others.

They shrieked and shouted but, except for the noise of water dashing and leaping between rocks, there was silence between us as we stared off into the distance.

I shut my eyes against the glare and felt my head loll back, heavy with the heat. When I opened them again, the boys had clambered out of the river. Panting and dripping wet, they flung themselves down near us, buried their shivering bodies in the warm sand and lay and giggled and whispered and squirmed until the sand made patterns and clung to them like the skin of a snake.

Tuthmosis turned his attention away from them and looked across at Anoukhet. 'What do you mean – we can't travel endlessly with the donkey men?'

She shrugged impatiently and disturbed two dragonflies that were darting and flitting about in jerky movements of flashing wings as they tried to settle on her arms and shoulders. 'We have to have a plan.'

'I *have* one.'

'What?' Anoukhet squinted through the sunlight at him.

Tuthmosis indicated upstream with his thumb. 'We have to go further south. There've been Egyptian garrisons in all these forts. Even here at Semna and Kumma. But they're the last forts. Beyond here, we come into the territory of the Kushites.'

I had a feeling of dread. We'd travelled so far

already. Thebes was like a dream from another life. 'Who are the Kushites?' I asked.

'Southern Nubians,' Anoukhet answered without looking up. One of the red dragonflies had settled on her shoulder like a tattoo. She was playing with a piece of grass – tickling a beetle as it crawled over the flakes of rock and at the same time trying to prevent Kyky from snatching it. It was a shiny creature with glassy wings and a silver-green body spotted with bronze. So beautiful, it could have been worn as a brooch.

Tuthmosis nodded. 'They're fierce warriors. Experts with bow and arrow and no fear of close combat and hand to hand struggle. They love nothing better than a skirmish. The land of Kush is rich in copper and gold and amethysts. My father wanted control over it but the Kushites wouldn't stand for it. They refuse to fall under Thebes. They hate the Egyptians.'

I glanced at him quickly. 'How will that help us? They'll know Anoukhet is Nubian but they'll see we're Egyptian.'

'I'll gather their support. Explain how my throne was stolen from me. And with them behind me, hit back at the Egyptian army. They hate Thebes. I'll have no difficulty in persuading the Kushites to act against Thebes.'

Anoukhet squinted back at him. 'Hah! They might act against Thebes but why should they help restore *you* as ruler of Egypt? And what if they don't believe you're a high-ranking prince – son of Amenhotep?'

'I'll have to prove who I am. They want a fair ruler as their neighbour. Not someone greedy like my father who threatened to take their gold, their lands and their women. I'll make a pact with them. An oath of promise.'

It seemed too easy. I looked out over the river. Three men were trying to swim their camels across a quieter stretch of water. The man in front held his camel's bridle rope in his mouth, urging him through the water while he swam alongside the moaning and grumbling beast. Behind this first camel, the others were tied head to tail and a man at the back did his best to keep them moving in the same direction against the current.

It was an almost impossible task. Like what lay ahead for us. But we were swimming against a fiercer and even riskier current. I glanced back at Tuthmosis. 'Do you think your word will stand?'

He shrugged. 'I'm the rightful King. My word is

the same as the word of Horus. I am the God-King.'

'Yes . . . but do the people in the Land of Kush honour the same gods?'

Tuthmosis clicked his tongue. He seemed impatient with me. Impatient that I should doubt him. 'The gods do not belong to Egypt alone. The people of Kush will see I'm a man of honour.'

Anoukhet shot a look at him. 'When will we leave to find the Kush army?'

'Tomorrow. Early.'

I glanced between them. 'So soon?'

Anoukhet swatted the dragonfly from her shoulder. 'We've waited too long. I'm ready for confrontation!'

Tuthmosis laughed. 'When are you *not* ready for confrontation, Anoukhet?'

We were distracted then by the boys who had crept closer towards us. They had discovered Kyky and wanted to play with her. A boy came up to show us how his chameleon's tongue could flick out to reach a dead fly on a piece of reed. A chameleon is truly imbued with magic. On the reed it was the greenest of green, yet the same chameleon turned murky against the dark skin of the boy's hand. The hot afternoon took on a lazy turn as we tested the chameleon against different colours and played and teased and pretended to chase the giggling boys.

If we had known then that they were spies, we might have behaved differently.

The nights next to the river had turned bitterly cold and I was grateful when Kyky snuggled between Anoukhet and me against my neck that night. The next morning, we stamped warmth back into our legs and began gathering our belongings. We thanked the donkey man and his companions for the time we'd spent together and, so as not to raise their suspicions, told them that news of a sick relative meant we had to return to Syene.

We were preparing to leave when the boys from the river came running to announce that soldiers were gathering just a short distance south in the desert.

'What sort of soldiers? Egyptian or Nubian?'

'Nubian.'

'Are you sure?'

The oldest of the boys nodded. 'My brother is a soldier with the Kushite army. I know these are Kushites. Their tunics have threads of red dye.'

Tuthmosis smiled. 'The time has come quicker than I thought.'

I took him by the arm. 'Is this the only way?'

'You can't lose heart now, Kara. Not after all this time. This is what we've come for. To take vengeance against Wosret!' He moved in closer and whispered, 'Just remember – until we know we can trust these Kushites, you must both behave like boys. Two women aren't safe mixed in with soldiers.' He looked between us. 'How good are you with bow and arrow?'

I shook my head. 'I've never used a bow and arrow.'

Anoukhet laughed as she slapped the dagger on her thigh. 'Don't be scared for my part, Tuthmosis. I'm as accurate with a bow as I am with my dagger. I can manage any bow and arrow – or any man for that matter!'

I saw her eyes flash and imagined she could. But when it came to men, I also knew the harsh truth of that time in the tent with Naqada. And a small catch of fear rippled through me like a moth fluttering against my ribcage. What if they found out we were women? What then?

We pulled on boots that were beginning to wear thin, gathered our meagre belongings and made sure our daggers were in our belts. I felt for my girdle bag to check I still had the Senet board and my mother's bronze mirror. The casket that Ta-Miu had filled with rose and cinnamon oil was long since empty, so I gave it to the boy to keep his chameleon in. Then we bade our farewells to the donkey men, left the river behind and trudged up the arid dunes ahead with Tuthmosis in the lead.

He and Anoukhet seemed glad to be moving on. But I hung back, fearing the moment we would meet the Kushite army. I should have noticed that the young boys hung back as well and did not accompany us. Fear is not enough to describe what I should have been feeling.

We'd been walking for some time when we reached the crest of the highest rise. Tuthmosis and Anoukhet both stopped dead in their tracks. I struggled to catch up with them. And then almost choked at what I saw.

From the rise opposite, right to the base of the valley and spread across as far as the eye could see in all directions, were soldiers. Hundreds upon hundreds of them. An entire encampment. The noise of them rose up like swarms of locusts feeding their way through a field, or angry hives of disturbed bees.

They stood crowded together, their dark, oiled bodies gleaming, quivers and bows slung across their backs, sunlight sparking off their metal spearheads and shining against their polished leather shields, looking as if they had just been forged in some fire-mine. Standing so densely packed together, they appeared hammered out of one mighty metal sheet that had spread itself over this dune and the next and the next, like a vast shield of beaten armour.

My heart seemed to stop. A cry escaped me and echoed out over the dunes.

In one very still moment everything went deathly quiet, as if every man had heard me. Standing exposed on the ridge of the dune, it seemed thousands of eyes turned to look at us.

CHAPTER TWENTY-ONE

MEN OF THE BOW

I felt my legs give way. Tuthmosis gripped me beneath my elbow and held me up.

'Be brave!' he whispered close to my ear. 'They're not enemies! They won't harm us! We must find their Commander.'

I nodded to show I had heard, but I could not speak.

A group of soldiers rushed towards us. I cringed and squeezed my eyes shut as I imagined the sound of arrows being drawn and the twang of bowstrings being pulled. But everything was confused. It happened so quickly I scarcely had time to draw breath and fill my lungs with air before we were surrounded and grabbed.

'Stop!' Tuthmosis shook himself free. 'I can prove—' but he was hit across the jaw before he could say more.

Anoukhet raised her dagger and showed no sign of putting it aside. She lunged in all directions before it was knocked from her hand. It skimmed the skin of a soldier's arm and left behind a bleeding gash.

'Keep still, curse you!' he shouted as he grabbed her and thrust her hands behind her back.

We were tied with rope and led down the soft sand between row upon row of bowmen who beat a slow, frightening tattoo against their shields and cursed into our faces. The heat and dust and raw smell of them terrified me. I could scarcely look up. The soldiers holding us shouted at them to make way. The men slowly parted but not without jeering and pulling at our cloaks and shoving us along so that I tripped and Anoukhet spat at one, and Kyky escaped from her cloak and went scampering off between them.

In the centre of the basin of arid dunes was an area barricaded with shields and staves to form an enclosure. We were shoved along through another horde of soldiers dressed in tunics woven with red thread and tied so tasselled fringes hung down in the front, wearing armbands of copper, gold and ivory

224

and studs of gold in their ears – every embellishment worn, it seemed, to make them appear more fierce and their bodies more powerful.

We passed between these masses and were taken through a wooden stave gateway. Inside the enclosure was an area which seemed more like an entire town. There were shelters for stores and weapons and tented areas, and in the centre a number of raised platforms stood on thick posts cut from trees, covered by large cloth canopies.

A man emerged from beneath one. His face twisted with disgust. 'Tie them up!' he bellowed.

'If we're separated,' Tuthmosis hissed as they jostled us along, 'keep to the truth of our story. Remember what I said. I have ways of proving—'

He was given a sharp thump across the back and his words ended in a groan.

'Keep quiet! The lot of you!' a soldier bellowed. 'Take that one away. Keep him apart. He has too much to say!'

They led Tuthmosis away and Anoukhet and I were tied each to a separate post of a platform.

'Hathor – Protector of Women ...' I begged, 'Goddess of the Moon ... Right Eye of Horus – protect me! Don't let them take Anoukhet away as well.'

'Shut up!' Anoukhet hissed. 'You'll only annoy them!'

I hadn't realised I'd spoken the words out loud. 'Where have they taken Tuthmosis?'

She shrugged and then called out to a soldier. 'Hey! You! We need water. And we need to speak to someone in authority!'

'You're prisoners. Prisoners can't make demands,' the soldier sneered back at her.

'What have we done to be made prisoners?'

'It's said you were planning an attack.'

'Three people were going to attack an army this size? Have you lost your senses?'

'It's what we've been told.'

'Who told you?'

'Boys from the river at the Belly of Stones. They spy on newcomers. They said you were whispering things.'

'They're only boys! Not spies! How would they know anything? They were mistaken. We weren't planning anything. We work for the donkey men.'

'Tell that to our leader.'

'Take us to him then. Or bring him here. Either way, I'll tell him.'

'I said before – you can't make demands!'

226

'I'm Nubian and so are you. I'm not making demands. I'm asking you as a fellow Nubian.'

'*You* might be Nubian, but the other two aren't. They're Egyptian and Egypt is the enemy.'

'Then all I ask is water. At least bring me that.'

When the soldier brought her a gourd, she whispered something to him. He threw back his head and laughed. Then he looked over his shoulder at me in surprise and came across and offered me a drink. He winked at Anoukhet and went away, laughing and shaking his head.

'What? What did you say, Anoukhet?'

'I said I was your slave.'

'My slave? How could that be?'

'I told him you were a high-ranking prince in disguise. That you bought me as your slave out of the kindness of your heart.'

'Tuthmosis said we should keep to the truth of our story.'

'I don't give a damn what he said! At least now we'll get some action. I said it was imperative I got help for you and that you would reward them. I asked him to call his leader to come and speak to us and I asked him to search for Kyky and my dagger as well.'

'But why was he laughing?'

'I had to give him some incentive. I told him I was a woman disguised as a man and there would be a reward for him but that he shouldn't tell my secret.'

'What?'

'What ...?' a loud, male voice echoed above us through the slatted platform at the same time. 'Am I to listen to a slave telling me what to do?'

'Not just an ordinary slave, sir. He says his master is an Egyptian prince. He hinted of some exchange. He spoke of the great wealth of the prince. That perhaps something could be arranged that was convenient to both sides.'

'Which one is the prince and which the slave? They both look like ragged dogs.'

The soldier came to the side of the platform and pointed below at us in turn. I looked up at the outline of the man above me but couldn't see the features of his face against the sunlight. He came down a wooden stairway and passed between us into the shadow, then stopped in front of Anoukhet and looked her directly in the face. She dropped her eyes. 'I'm not the prince, sir. He's there.' She indicated to me.

With that the man turned to look at me. He wore the same tunic and the same armbands of gold, copper and ivory, with a belt of cowrie shells and a short Nubian wig, yet even though his skin was dark and sunburnt, I could see he wasn't Nubian.

He narrowed his eyes in the half light as he looked at me and I stared back at him. For a moment his face seemed to pale. But perhaps it was only the shadowed light beneath the platform. He swirled around and commanded a soldier, 'Cut them loose!'

'But—?'

'Do as I say!' Then he sent the soldiers away and marched Anoukhet and I up the stairs ahead of him and wrenched the canopy aside so that we entered a small, enclosed tented area hung with fighting instruments – bows, arrows, daggers and finely-honed axes and spears with such sharp-pointed blades I shuddered at the thought of them piercing my body.

I turned to look at the man. Around his neck I saw a glint of blue glass. It was a common sort of amulet. Anyone could have bought a similar one in any marketplace. But then my heart skipped a beat. I saw the dreadful scar that marked his shoulder. Strapped to the stump of his right arm was a false limb made of wood.

'Can it be . . .?' I whispered. I reached out to touch the blue glass amulet at his neck.

He wrenched my hand aside. 'Stand back!' he commanded.

But I had seen. It *was* a scorpion. 'Katep . . .? Can it be? Is that truly you? Do you not know me?'

He took me by the shoulders and studied my face for a long time, as if he wanted to be completely sure.

'Isikara?'

CHAPTER TWENTY-TWO

KATEP

I stood staring at my brother in complete disbelief, taking in the details of his weatherworn face.

He looked me up and down. 'Isikara! What are you doing dressed like this?' Then glanced across at Anoukhet. 'And who is this boy?'

I was surprised at the coldness in his voice. But then for the moment I'd forgotten – we were still in disguise.

I glanced across at her. The sun shining through a gap in the canopy struck her oiled skin and the crop of gleaming dark curls that were beginning to grow again. She was standing lounging against a post, taking in the scene between Katep and me – her eyes not missing a thing. There was an easy and comfortable look to her stance. With her legs stretched out in that indifferent, confident manner of hers and with her short curls and cloak, she *did* seem like a boy.

A very handsome boy at that, with her flashing eyes and dark hair and her lean, lithe body and long dancer's legs. Yes, it suited her well. Suddenly I could see why Katep was taking the stance of a protective brother. He was jealous and suspicious of me being in the company of such a handsome boy.

He squared his body to face Anoukhet. 'Don't just stand there. What have you to say for yourself? What are you to my sister? Why are you travelling with her?'

Anoukhet smiled across at him. 'She's my friend.'

'I can see that! But what is your relationship? And why have you taken up with her? What are your intentions?'

'Katep—' I tried to interrupt but he held up his hand to stop me.

'My intention is to remain true to her all my life,' Anoukhet replied with a half-smile on her face. I could see she was teasing him.

He glanced back at me. 'What does this mean, Isikara?'

I couldn't stop myself from giggling. 'Katep ... Anoukhet is a woman!'

'*What?*' He strode across to her and pulled her towards a shaft of sunlight coming in through the canopy and fumbled with her cloak.

'Stop! You can't disrobe her! Believe me – she's a woman. Trust me. You don't need proof. She's my true friend and we've come safely through this ordeal together only by both being disguised as boys.'

But Anoukhet had already opened her cloak to reveal the swell of her bosoms. I saw the colour rise in Katep's cheeks as he quickly stepped back and looked away in confusion. 'A woman! What will the Commander say about having a woman in the camp?' Then he looked across at me. '*Two* women in the camp.'

I felt the colour rise in my cheeks now. Katep would never have referred to me as a woman before. He must have seen some difference in me.

'This is an impossible situation. There'll be a riot if they know there are women here and that one of them is my sister. It's a camp of hardened soldiers. They behave like soldiers: they swear and curse and don't always bathe. They're a rough bunch.'

Anoukhet smiled back at him. 'I can swear and curse with the best of them.'

'It's impossible. You can't remain here! What about

the other boy? The one being held separately because he was causing trouble. Is *he* a girl too? Am I to tell my Commander there are *three* women in the camp?'

Suddenly I thought of Tuthmosis. In the relief of discovering Katep, I had forgotten about him. Now I felt myself blushing even more as I caught Anoukhet's eyes and saw she was laughing at my confusion. 'No.' I shook my head. 'He's not a girl. He's the Crown Prince Tuthmosis of Egypt.'

Katep shot a look at us. 'What? You're travelling with the Crown Prince Tuthmosis? There was rumour he'd been murdered.' He turned quickly to me. 'Why are you so far from Thebes? Why are you not with Father?'

'Have you not heard what happened in Thebes?

He turned abruptly and strode through the canopy and stood with his back to us at the railings. 'So the rumours are true?'

I went across to him and touched his shoulder.

He spun around angrily. 'Get back before anyone sees you! Is it true? Was Father poisoned? Was it Wosret's doing?'

'I'll tell you everything. But first order your men to free Tuthmosis.'

'They're not *my* men to order about. I'm just

the leader of a phalanx under the orders of a Commander.'

Anoukhet shrugged. 'Speak to whoever you have to. But ask them to find my dagger and Kyky as well.'

'Kyky?'

'My monkey.'

Katep sighed. 'Two women, a prince and a monkey! The Commander will *never* allow this!'

He shouted to the soldiers below. Then he pointed for us to sit on some cushions on the floor.

'But Katep, why didn't you go to Sinai? Why are you here in Nubia?'

He shrugged. 'It's easier for a man with only one arm to sail rather than row. The winds took me south and I kept going.'

'I thought I'd never see you again.'

'I thought the same thing. I was angry. I left without saying a proper farewell to Father.'

'He understood your anger. He knew why you left.'

'When did you last see him?'

'In the royal wabet chamber. He said he would follow.'

'He might still come.'

'It's been too long.'

'But he might—'

'No, Katep—'

We interrupted one another in our hurry to hear what the other was saying, while Anoukhet looked from one to another and every now and again added her own words. Every time she spoke, Katep looked at her with complete attention. I could see by the way his eyes lingered that he was already smitten. So by the time Tuthmosis arrived, sat down and began his side of the story, Katep gave him a curt bow and impatiently hurried him along, keen to turn back to Anoukhet and hear the words from her lips instead.

'Tell me about this Naqada.'

'A scorpion.'

'You're Nubian.'

'From Syene.'

I'd never seen my brother like this. I thought I knew him like the blood in my own veins, but this was a different Katep. His eyes barely left her face.

Then a soldier came with Kyky and brought a message as well. Suddenly Katep seemed reminded of his role. He stood up and began pacing. 'It's impossible! You can't stay! The Commander will never allow it.'

'Why not?'

'How can he allow Egyptians in his camp? Egyptians are the enemy.'

'He allowed you!'

'That was different. I'm a mercenary. I fight alongside whoever will pay me.'

Tuthmosis nodded. 'We will too.'

'But you're not just any Egyptian. You're the son of his most vile enemy, Amenhotep!'

'But with the Nubians on my side I can defeat Wosret and my brother. When I'm King, the Nubians will be free of oppression. They'll never fear another attack from Egypt. What is theirs will remain theirs. This I promise.'

Katep shrugged. 'Perhaps we can persuade him. But if he agrees you'll have to work. Every person in camp has a job to do.' He glanced at Tuthmosis. 'And you'll have to obey commands.'

I could see he found it hard to believe this person – dressed in tatters, smelling of donkeys and camels – was a royal personage.

'The men won't stand for airs and graces. Even from one who is the son of a pharaoh. Perhaps more so, when he's the son of a pharaoh! You'll need to earn their trust.'

As he sized Tuthmosis up and down, I saw him take

in the weak leg, puckered with scars, and saw him involuntary touch his own false limb. I saw Tuthmosis's eyes drawn to the wooden arm but he didn't comment. Katep picked up the look and a dark flash of annoyance crossed his face.

I glanced between them. I wanted them to like one another. 'Tuthmosis could be of use to the Kushite army. He was a charioteer. He went hunting with his father. They hunted lion.'

Tuthmosis shook his head. 'You don't have to speak up for me, Kara. And it was my father who hunted lion, not me.'

'A charioteer?' I could tell Katep was impressed. 'I would give anything to have our army equipped with chariots, but we've no means of getting horses or chariots so far south along the river.'

Tuthmosis nodded. 'Chariots put you in a position of attack – right into the heart of the battle.'

Suddenly Katep was on the defence again. 'But the Egyptians keep their charioteers as the elite of their army. Only the elite have special bows, while the rest of their foot soldiers carry ordinary bows. With us, *all* our men carry special bows. We win through our skill and expert marksmanship – not through privilege and status.'

I exchanged glances with Katep. He was being argumentative. And he knew I knew. The thread that bound us like a spider's web was still intact. I knew him so well. He was testing Tuthmosis.

Tuthmosis eyed him. 'I'm a good marksman. Steady with a bow. But I've never killed a man.'

I turned away then. I was afraid to hold Katep's glance because of the secret that lay between the rest of us. I hadn't told him the details of Naqada's end — that I had killed a man!

Katep narrowed his eyes. 'Are you a coward, then?'

'There's never been a need for me to kill a man. Have you?' Tuthmosis responded.

Katep shrugged. 'I told you . . . I'm a mercenary. I work for the underdog. I kill where I have to.'

It was as if these two were on warring sides. Fighting some strange hand to hand duel. I interrupted quickly. 'But how did you come to be leader of a Kushite phalanx?'

'Because of my bow skills. The Commander was swimming in the Great River one day. I was passing in my boat when a crocodile appeared from nowhere and lunged at him. The crocodile had him in its jaws when I killed it with my arrow — using my false arm.'

It was the first time he had referred to the wooden arm-piece he wore. Then, as if to break the tension, he nodded across at Anoukhet, who was comforting Kyky. 'I know Isikara has no bow skills. What are yours?'

She tossed her head and laughed. 'My skills? Hah! If I had my dagger, I'd show you. And I'm as accurate with a bow as I am with a dagger. I'll manage as well as any man.'

Her reply made Katep defensive again. 'It's not as easy as you think. We use the composite bow. It's strengthened with horn. You need power in your shoulders to bend it back.'

Anoukhet needed no further challenge. 'I'm strong enough!' In one quick movement, she sprang forward and grabbed a bow from the side of the tent. She chose an arrow, fitted it to the string, then strode to the canopy opening, pulled the sinew back until the bow-ends curved sharply and the feathers touched her breast, took aim and released. It shot out over the heads of the soldiers below and came to rest squarely in the wood of one of the upright posts of the enclosure.

When she turned, her eyes challenged Katep's.

'Come here!' he demanded.

She got up close and stood so there was barely the space of a hand between their faces.

He looked directly into her eyes. Then he gripped her wrist with his good hand and held it so hard I could see her skin whiten around the edge of his fingers. 'That was *my* bow. Don't *ever* remove my bow from its hook again without being asked.'

I waited for Anoukhet to toss her head and spit out one of her taunts. But instead she looked down. And when Katep released her wrist, she turned and placed the bow carefully back on its hook.

I suspect Katep realised his victory because he went on quickly. 'I'll speak to my Commander. It's up to him whether you stay or not.' He looked directly at Anoukhet. 'But you can't behave as you please. You have to take orders.' Then he turned to me and spoke as if I was still his little sister, stuck up in the fork of the mimosa tree. 'And you can't suddenly become scared. In battle there's blood and people dying. It's dangerous and terrifying.'

I threw my shoulders back and held my head high as I met his eye. 'I'm prepared to fight. I'm not scared of blood! I helped Father with embalming, remember.' But as soon as the words left my mouth, I knew there was no truth in them. I may have helped with embalming, but I *was* scared of blood. I'd seen Katep's blood when the crocodile tore his arm and I had been terrified. And I'd seen Naqada's blood on my hands too. The horrible blackness of it in the moonlight.

I thought of the moment when I had hunted Naqada. When I'd been a lynx. Perhaps that's what being in the army was like. You had to forget everything. You had to fight with the instinct of a hunting animal. It was kill . . . or be killed. A lynx wouldn't have worried about blood.

I had done it for Anoukhet then. Now I would do it for Tuthmosis. And for the revenge of my father. For the honour of his name.

Katep shook his head as if he'd read my thoughts. 'The Commander won't put women into battle. You'll have to practise your bow skills and your spear throwing, but only for your own protection. Your work will be in the kitchen, preparing meals and seeing the bread is baked and the rations are good. Men can't fight on empty stomachs.'

'What?' I looked at him in disbelief. Then I tossed my head. 'That might be so . . . but their stomachs won't be filled by *me*! I'm not going into the kitchen just because I'm a woman!'

242

'You might be a woman but you're also a soldier now, and soldiers have to take orders.'

'*You* might be a phalanx leader but you're also my brother! And brothers are not always obeyed.'

Katep narrowed his eyes. 'Father was right.'

'About what?'

'About you! You're stubborn, obstinate and impossible!'

'So will you ask your Commander if I can train alongside the men?'

Katep groaned then regarded me steadily. With a sigh, he responded, 'Yes . . . but—'

'Katep!' I lunged at him before he could go on, wrapping my arms around him and hugging him tightly.

He pulled away roughly, his face reddening as he glanced at Anoukhet, who was smiling. 'You might be allowed to train alongside the men but whether you go into battle is another matter. The Commander will decide.'

I was too busy laughing and hugging him to listen. 'Oh, Katep! I found you! After all this time, I've found you!'

Kyky sensed the excitement and started bounding around the platform as well.

243

'Kara ... wait ... please!' He held off my hands. 'I must first speak with the Commander. I've built up his trust but I'll need to persuade him to take the three of you on.'

Anoukhet tossed her head. 'I don't want to be treated differently. Why not just remain silent? You don't have to reveal that we're girls, nor do you have to reveal Tuthmosis's identity. Let the Commander think we're Nubian boys come to join the Kushite army!'

Katep shook his head. 'Because you're not all three Nubian, and the Kushites work on truth. The Commander must know the truth from the start. It's for him to decide whether you stay or not.'

I glanced at him quickly. 'You mean he might not agree? But that's impossible! We can't be parted again so soon.'

He shrugged. 'It's not just a question of the two of you being girls, it's the question of having a prince of Egypt – the *enemy* – amongst us.'

Tuthmosis shook his head. 'I'm not an enemy of the Kush. The Kingdom of Kush and I have the *same* enemy – the murdering usurpers who have seized my throne. I want my Kingdom back and I'll fight to get it by any means. Even if I have to first defeat my own

Egyptian army. The Egyptians are under the orders of the traitor, Wosret!'

'The Commander will need to be persuaded of this. And you'll have to prove you're the son of Amenhotep, the rightful Crown Prince.'

My hands dropped to my side. Suddenly I was fearful. 'He can't do that! What if he *does* prove he's the son of Amenhotep? Your Commander could decide to kill him. As you said – Egypt is the enemy.'

Katep shook his head. 'I give you my word. If Tuthmosis can prove his Kingship, we might be able to persuade the Commander that by making his brother illegally King, the High Priests of Thebes have once more proved that the greed, corruption and power of Egypt needs to be stopped. The Commander doesn't want the land of Kush to become Egypt's vassal so that Egypt can claim all her riches – her gold and copper and ivory and ebony. He wants war with Egypt. This will give him his excuse.'

I turned to Tuthmosis. 'How can you prove who you are? You carry no identity. Your cloak and broad-collar were left on the other boy in the royal wabet chamber in Thebes.'

Katep glanced at him. 'Is there nothing?'

'I've kept this.' Tuthmosis removed something from his girdle bag. 'My royal pectoral. It has my insignia on it.'

I glanced at him. 'But you had nothing when we left the chamber. How did you come by it?' Our eyes met. Then I looked away quickly. I felt foolish. Of course, Ta-Miu had given it to him at the Palace. She had handed him something as we were leaving. But why had *she* been keeping it?

Katep ran his fingers over the fine gold filigree with its lapis lazuli, turquoise and carnelian inlays of two falcons clutching Tuthmosis's name in a cartouche. The cartouche itself rested on the largest green emerald I had ever seen. It was in the shape of a sacred scarab. The one who rolls the great Sun across the sky. The heart amulet of a king.

'This will do. Hurry then. It's better that the two of you remain here while Tuthmosis and I speak to the Commander. Hang it around your neck, Tuthmosis, so all will know who you are.'

Anoukhet looked sceptical. 'What's to stop anyone thinking it was stolen? An emerald that size would be worth stealing. And dressed like this, he looks more like a scruffy thief than a prince.'

'I have a tattoo on my upper thigh that shows

the same insignia,' Tuthmosis said as he followed after Katep.

I spun around to face her when they'd left. 'What do you think?'

She raised her eyebrow and looked at me quizzically. 'Do you mean – do I think they're stupid not to take us with them to the Commander?'

'No, of course not! You know that's not what I'm asking. I mean, what do you think of Katep?'

She turned away and marched up and down, pretending to inspect the bows and weapons.

'Well?'

'He's interesting,' was her only reply. Then she spun around with a mischievous sparkle in her eye. 'But it's not just *us* who'll have to prove ourselves. *He'll* have to prove himself to *me* too. Let's see what he's like in battle.'

By the time Katep and Tuthmosis returned, the sun had set over the desert and the soldiers were already lighting their fires as the cool green light of evening crept up.

'So? What did he say?' I asked as they stepped through the opening of the canopy.

'Well?' Anoukhet stood in front of them with her arms folded. 'Can we stay?'

Katep shook his head. 'Tuthmosis can remain but—'

'What about us?'

He shook his head. 'Not the two of you.'

'What? Why not? Why should it be any different?'

Then he laughed. 'Not until the men in my phalanx have decided about having two girls in their camp. It's my phalanx who'll have to put up with you.'

Anoukhet's eyes flashed as Katep left the canopy again and went out to speak to his men. 'Hah! *Put up with us!*'

But I knew Katep was teasing her.

We tried to listen as best we could but we couldn't hear most of what was being discussed. At one point there was raucous laughter when I heard Katep say it was Anoukhet who had shot the arrow into the post.

A single voice bellowed out, 'She's a damn fine shot, then!' Then there were other, angry shouts.

'But she's Nubian. She's from Syene,' Katep argued.

We could hear differences of opinion and some disputes and a few 'No! No . . . no . . .'s then some more boisterous laughter.

Then we heard Katep's steps on the wooden stairs. His face was serious as he entered the canopied tent.

'I told them you were useless with a bow and arrow, Kara.'

I glared back at him. 'Only a brother could be so brutally honest. Could you not say how skilled I was with a throwstick?'

'How would a throwstick help in battle? You'd fell one man and then what? Your weapon would be gone!'

'So what was their answer then?' Anoukhet demanded.

Katep couldn't keep a straight face any longer. He broke into a broad grin and then burst out laughing. He gave Anoukhet a mock bow and handed her the lost dagger. 'It was decided on the strength of your bowshot and by the quality of the dagger you carry, that you both can stay.'

I should have been cross with Katep for making me appear so useless but instead I clasped him about the neck. He pulled my hands away. 'Behave yourself, Isikara. You're a soldier now.'

CHAPTER TWENTY-THREE

FLETCHING

So it was settled. Anoukhet and I began training along-side the men in earnest but all the time I was mindful of Katep's warning that we wouldn't go into battle and that we were learning skills merely for our own protection.

I sensed it wasn't easy for Tuthmosis.

'The Kushites will want to use you as their pawn,' Katep warned. 'You'll have to convince them you can be trusted. They'll protect you, but only if you give them what they want – freedom from the yoke of Egypt.'

Eventually, after their initial resentment, it was

Tuthmosis's strength and ability with a bow that won the soldiers over.

For Anoukhet and me it was different. The men looked sceptical at the idea of two girls handling bows. They treated us as something of a novelty, like two exotic animals that belonged in a palace menagerie rather than an army camp. As if we were strange creatures that couldn't quite be trusted to behave as expected, and they sent us furtive looks and watched our every movement.

Katep gave up his canopied platform room for us to sleep in. So, after dark we were left alone. But by daylight we were soldiers alongside the others and we knew we had to work hard to earn their trust and friendship.

Each morning we assembled before the sun had risen, with goosebumps on our arms, and stood shivering in rows while our phalanx was inspected by Katep. If a bow wasn't oiled to a gleam or properly strung with the right sinew, or an arrowhead was blunt, or a strap of a quiver worn or the grip of a shield frayed, we were punished alongside the rest of the men and made to do extra camp duties. It made no difference that we were women. In fact, I sensed

Katep was harder on us because he was my brother.

The only exercise we escaped was pulling heavy posts through the sand by thongs tied to our heads, to strengthen the back muscles. I was grateful for this. But we were expected to take part in sword sparring against heavy bollards hung from poles, javelin throwing until my arm felt it would fall off and axe techniques that left me terrified and speechless.

Katep took it upon himself to personally train us with the composite bow, standing next to us, hour after hour, demonstrating the stance and the pull. He had relearned his skills, and pulled the bowstring with his left hand now. He used the wooden right limb, with its pronged fork at the end, to hold the curve of the bow. He was well equipped to teach us. But there was a lot to remember.

'Relax, Kara. Bend your knees. Don't hold the bow arm straight out. Have it slightly bent at the elbow. And don't throttle the bow with your grip. When you draw back, keep an anchor point at your cheek. A tooth that you touch with your bow fingers so you mark the place you pull back to.'

He showed me no sisterly favouritism. In fact there were days when my body was so tired I hated him for it and I almost begged to go on kitchen duty. But

I realised it was for our own safety that he took so much trouble to admonish me.

'Draw back harder, Isikara. Lay your body into the bow. Use your back muscles. A bowman's aim is to pull the sinew so hard that the tips of the bow-ends almost meet. You have to have power in your back and legs – like Anoukhet.'

'Curse you, Anoukhet! It's easier for you with your dancer's legs!' I hissed under my breath at her as I squinted against the glare and struggled yet again to pull back the taut sinew, until my back, shoulders and arms ached with fatigue.

The bows were stiff and made of wood and polished ibex horn, and stood almost sixteen hands high – much more than the height of a man. Fine, for someone as tall and strong as Anoukhet, but impossible for me.

In the evenings, sprawled out on my mat, in the privacy of our canopy, away from the glances of the men, I ranted. 'I hate this! And I hate Katep! I'll never be a bowman!'

Anoukhet smiled. 'Come, let me rub oil into your shoulders and arms. It'll ease the pain in your muscles.'

'It's not just the pain in my shoulders and arms – every part of my body aches! And there are blisters on my hands. My thumb and middle finger are worn raw from pulling back the sinew. I can't go on!'

It was Tuthmosis who showed me sympathy instead of Katep.

He came one evening and brought me two stone rings. 'Wear them on your forefinger and middle finger to take the full brunt of pulling back the arrow.'

Anoukhet's eyes sparkled. 'How romantic you are – bringing stone rings instead of jewelled ones!'

He chose to ignore her, but returned the following evening to ask if they had helped. 'I want to show you something. Come.' He took me by the hand and led me past the soldiers' fires to the far side of the camp, where an old man was boiling two cauldrons of foul-smelling brew.

'Not supper, I hope?'

Tuthmosis smiled and held out his hand. 'This is Kha. He's been making bows and arrows all his life. I've asked Katep if you can be his assistant.'

I flashed a look at him. 'What? So it *is* cooking you've set me up with, after all!'

The old man eyed me. 'It's horn and bone we're boiling, not food. Horn of ibex, boiled to soften it so as to bind it to the wooden bow for extra strength and flexibility.' He nodded at the other cauldron. 'And those are hare bones, boiling to make a sticky stew that keeps the layers of bone and wood together. The jelly also holds the cover bindings of thin bark or sinew in place so that everything is glued together tightly. The stickier the stew, the better.'

He sized me up and down. 'Longbows are difficult to make, especially composite bows. You don't look strong enough! Indeed, there's a rumour in the camp that you're a woman. But that matters not to me. My days of chasing after women are long gone.' He chuckled toothlessly.

'She's skilful with her hands. She'll be good at bow-making,' said Tuthmosis.

The old man frowned at me from under his thick brows. 'Once you make a mistake – and you'll make plenty – you have to throw the bow away and start again. There's no sense in finishing a bow that's already scuppered, that you know won't shoot properly. A bow needs respect.'

I looked from him to Tuthmosis. 'I've never done anything like this before . . . I'm not sure . . .'

The old man sighed heavily. 'All you need is a wood shaper and a sharp carving knife, strong fingers and patience. Sit down.' He indicated a place at his fire for both of us.

I moved so that I was upwind of the steam and stench of the boiling cauldrons.

'Bow skills are governed by how good your bow is. A good bowman should always be able to make his *own* bow and arrows. None of these young men know a thing about bow-making. If I were their Commander I would force them each to make their own. But I'm old and no one takes any notice of me.'

He began to demonstrate with his gnarled, callused hands. 'The horn of an ibex is split down the centre into two halves and the outside worked smooth and shaved down. By boiling the horn and then clamping it down, it stays flat once cooled. Then the horn piece is shaved into thin strips to fit the bow-piece. The strips are covered with hare-bone paste and clamped against the bow and left to dry. The purpose is to make the bow flexible. To allow the archer to pull it back further, without breaking the wood.' He scowled at me. 'Do you understand that?'

I nodded.

'A bowman is a musician.'

'A musician?'

He nodded. 'It's not about brute force.'

Not about brute force? Katep should hear this!

The old man ran his fingers along a bow. 'A bowman

256

must know what his bow can do. Know exactly how much tension it can take. His hands must be as sensitive as a butterfly's antennae. Each shiver must be felt as keenly as a quiver in a lute string. When a bowstring is pulled, energy is stored in the bow limb. When the sinew is released the energy is transferred to the feathered arrow. It's all very simple.'

I nodded even though I knew it wasn't so simple.

'Let me see your hands.'

I held them out to him.

'Hmmm . . . long slender fingers, sensitive enough to be a musician. But I see you have blisters!' He scowled again and shook his head. 'I can't have you carving horn when you already have blisters.'

'So then what . . .?'

He squinted back at me. 'Are you any good at bringing wildfowl down?'

Tuthmosis nodded. 'She's superb with a throwstick.'

'I'll tell you what then . . . you can search for arrow feathers for me. I'm getting too old and tired to be bringing down wildfowl and plucking feathers to make arrows for the troops. You'll make a good fletcher.'

'A fletcher?' I looked from Tuthmosis to the old man.

He nodded. 'The process of attaching the feather flights to the shaft of an arrow is called fletching. In battle we need hundreds of arrows. Each man must have a full quota in his quiver. Without good arrows an archer is nothing.'

Tuthmosis's eyes searched mine, waiting for my answer. He had done this for my sake. He knew I was struggling to master the bow and had found me an easier job that would make me feel I was still part of camp life. I smiled across at him and nodded.

The old man eyed me. 'So it's settled, then. Every day you'll report for duty and fill your quota of arrows for the day. And if the sun has set and you've not made the required number, you'll work into the night by firelight. There's no dragging your feet here.'

And so it was that Anoukhet became an archer, spending most of her days training alongside Katep, and I became a fletcher.

From under the awning of the old man's workshop – sitting as far away from the stench of the boiling cauldrons as I could – I sometimes spotted the two of them with their heads together, deep in conversation, or Katep standing close behind her, guiding her shoulders and her arms, and repositioning her head as she took aim. And sometimes too, in the late afternoons when the sun had lost its sting, I caught sight of them walking out into the desert, their heads close together, and I knew then it wasn't just bow skills they were discussing.

Each morning I woke early and went out with my throwstick into the dunes before sunrise, in search of small falcon and quail and guinea fowl. Sometimes I went as far as the river to bring down waterfowl. Then I strung the fowl together and carried them back to camp and plucked them well before handing them over to the cooks to add to the day's meal. The best feathers for fletching were the stiff tail and wing feathers. These I sorted and tied into bundles according to their patterns.

The arrows I made were unmistakable.

Because of my long forays out each day, I collected wild herbs, grasses, bulbs and fragrant leaves for the cooks as well. I soon discovered from carrying them together with the wildfowl, that some plant juices stained and it was possible to colour the feathers. From the crushed root of alkanet, I made red dye. From safflower thistles, I made yellow. I boiled the dyes and carefully steeped the feathers in them so that the white parts between the dark stripes and patterns took up the colours. Then the feathers were laid out to dry. Afterwards I trimmed then with a sharp knife and slotted them into grooves I had cut in the tail-ends of fine straight saplings.

I was pleased with my work. So was the old bow-maker. I could tell this when he held my arrows up without comment and peered down their length to see they were true. They were fine arrows, well-made, each with their own distinctive, unique colouring. I had put my mark on them. The archers were well pleased too. Soon each phalanx asked for their own particular colour and pattern combination, and each man branded his own arrow shafts with his personal signet.

The arrows I made for Tuthmosis were different to all the others. For him, I chose feathers that were the more difficult to find – completely white with no markings so that the white took the dye entirely. Wing feathers from spoonbills, white egrets and storks. But they were larger birds and more difficult to bring down.

There was a beetle, that if squeezed, gave off a bluish paste. If Tuthmosis couldn't wear the Blue Khepresh Warrior Crown in battle, he could at least have arrows of the royal colour. Heavenly blue for eternity and life, to mark his royalty and divinity. And secretly, also heavenly blue to mark him as being as handsome as the God of the Blue Lotus, Nefertem.

I saw Katep make note of this but not say anything. So I made his arrows with entirely red feathers. A dark, solid red. A link to bravery and fire. The colour of life and victory. And I coloured Anoukhet's arrow feathers green. Green for proof of her power and her friendship. Green because it is the colour of joy and rebirth. And to the tail-ends of them I added tiny shreds of red ribbon to tie up evil and also as a sign of her bravery.

The old man Kha instructed me to make the arrow-heads with small barbed flints instead of bronze.

'Flint is harder than bronze and will not bend or flatten if it strikes bone. Even if the wound is not immediately fatal, flint-heads that are barbed and bound to the shaft so that the head dislodges from the shaft when someone tries to withdraw it, causing the wound to fester and be fatal.'

I shuddered. 'It sounds barbaric!'

'All war is barbaric!'

I nodded. 'War is not something a woman would easily dream up!'

Yet I was wrong. I thought of Hathor and her double image, Sekhmet – the Lioness of War. The Fighting

Goddess. The one who helps the king vanquish his enemies in battle. The lionesses of Sekhmet lined the pathway to the Temple of Karnak – put there by Tuthmosis's father.

CHAPTER TWENTY-FOUR

THE EGYPTIAN ARMY

The tips of my fingers became calloused and strong with cutting and shaping the arrows. The days passed quickly, with me searching for dyes and feathers and sitting alongside the old man, Kha, listening to him telling stories of great battles and bravery. So when Katep unexpectedly called Tuthmosis, Anoukhet and me to his tent one night, I felt my heart slip into my throat as I sensed that the rhythm of my days was about to change.

'Spies have informed the Commander that the Egyptian army has encamped a short distance from here. They've travelled from the southern fortresses by boat, intent on war and forcing the boundaries of Egypt further south. But this is not their full objective.'

I glanced quickly at him. 'What is it then?'

'They're using the southern boundary as an excuse. They've been sent by Wosret.'

'How do you know?'

'Why else would they leave the forts and come so far south now? Your brother's too young to be planning war.' He turned to look at Tuthmosis and shook his head. 'No. Word must've got out and travelled back to Thebes. Wosret must know you are here with the Kushite army.'

I glanced across at Tuthmosis. This was what he wanted, but now the time had come, I was terrified.

'Their camp is set up beyond some cliffs to the north of here, alongside the river. Their chariots are lined up – too many to count. The Commander has asked me to scrutinise the camp secretly so we can make immediate plans for attack.'

Tuthmosis eyed him. 'I'll go with you.'

'Me too!' Anoukhet said.

Katep shook his head. 'It's too risky. Only Tuthmosis must come. He knows Egyptian strategy. How they will use their chariots. How they will organise their troops. Timing is essential. We need to strike within hours, while they're still resting from their long journey.'

'Within hours? So soon?' Despite the weeks of training, suddenly I felt ill with fear.

Katep caught my eye and nodded. 'We have to take them by surprise. Unprepared. Their chariots will be difficult to manoeuvre into position in the confined space between the river and cliff.'

Orders were given to douse all the campfires and Anoukhet and I sat hugging our knees to our chests in the darkness as we watched Katep and Tuthmosis set out. They carried no torches but in the moonlight we could still see them creeping from the shadow of one dune to the next.

Suddenly Anoukhet jumped up. 'I can't bear this. I'm going after them.'

'No! You heard what Katep said. It's too risky!'

'Are you coming too or not? Quickly, make up your mind before we lose sight of them.'

The soft sand muffled our footfalls as we ran after the two of them. When we saw their dark shadows pause near the crest of a sand dune ahead, we lay down on our stomachs and wriggled forward like snakes.

'What do you see?' Anoukhet whispered as we came up alongside them.

Katep's head whipped around. 'I told you to stay behind.'

'I'm not some pet dog to be trained!'

'Go back to camp,' he hissed.

'We're here now, and besides—'

'Sshh then!' Katep put his hand across her mouth. 'Just keep silent and do as I say! Keep back now!' He edged forward on his elbows and peered over the crest. Then he beckoned Tuthmosis to do the same. We crept closer as well.

An icy shiver went through me as I looked down. A carpet of soldiers spread out from the base of the cliffs right down to the river, their fires making as many stars as were in the sky. Their helmets, and their weapons of spear and sword and the linked armoury on their bodies caught the moonlight and reflected back flashes of silver in every direction. And, as if to magnify their force, their armoury reverberated with a sharp metallic clinking, more menacing than musical.

Behind them, right against the cliffs, row upon row of golden chariots turned silver in the moonlight. Even from where I lay, I could see the double crown of Egypt emblazoned on their sides and the powerful horses cast like statues of molten silver, grazing from fodder bags lying on the sand.

I could not control the shivers that ran through me. Anoukhet wriggled alongside and squeezed my hand.

Katep pinched up some sand with his fingers and let it blow so he could tell the direction of the wind. He whispered to Tuthmosis. 'The wind is in our favour to get up close. I need to be sure of their weapons.' Then he turned to us. 'The two of you stay here. Don't dare follow! Use the call of the fiery-necked nightjar to warn us if necessary.' And with that they were gone – ghostly shadows, sneaking down the dune alongside the cliffs.

'The fiery-necked nightjar?' I whispered into Anoukhet's ear. I could hardly control the chattering of my teeth. 'Do you know the call?'

In the moonlight I saw her smile and nod. 'Good Horus . . . deliver us! Good Horus . . . deliver us!' she whispered back.

They seemed to be gone for ever. We watched and waited while the fires burned down and the men began to settle for the night. The sand was cold. A chill wind had sprung up. I felt for the cowrie shell and moonstone eye at my throat and listened to the strange night calls. The desert seemed more threatening by moonlight. We heard no call of a fiery-necked nightjar but from somewhere came the long, eerie shriek of a desert hyena that sent shudders through me. I longed to be safely back at the camp.

Anoukhet wriggled her body to get more comfortable. 'It's damn cold. I wish I'd gone with them.' She took a leather flask from her girdle bag, pulled the stopper and took a gulp. 'Have some!'

It was palm wine. I felt the warmth of it in my throat and knew I needed another sip to steady my nerves and bring back feeling into my arms and legs.

Eventually, when the moon disappeared behind a cloud, there was a movement ahead. Two figures loomed up out of the shadows. For a moment my heart stopped. Then I saw it was Katep and Tuthmosis.

'What took you so long?' Anoukhet hissed.

'We had to wait for cloud cover. The moon was too bright to make a dash for it. Let's go! Hurry now!'

When we were back in camp, the Commander called a meeting with Katep, Tuthmosis and the other phalanx leaders. The men assembled a little way from the encampment, and sat together in a small clearing. Anoukhet and I followed and crouched, listening at a distance, as they made plans.

'So? What weapons did they have?'

'The usual. Some fine-looking daggers. Bronze-headed spears. Plenty of khopesh swords with sickle blades which don't seem too well-honed. Looks more as if they'll use them as blunt, chopping instruments. They'll break a neck easily. Or crush a windpipe with a good swing.'

I swallowed hard. There was nothing I wanted to hear less.

Tuthmosis spoke hurriedly. 'Their deadliest weapon is the chariot with an archer, handpicking his targets at speed. The chariots are light and open-backed with just a handrail for balance; and they have the stronger, six-spoke wheel, ideal for rough ground but difficult to manoeuvre in soft sand.'

Katep nodded. 'Their major mistake is that they've used the cliffs as a hiding place for the chariots, instead of encircling the camp with them for protection. If we attack, the chariots are deep behind their foot soldiers instead of out in front. They've still to harness the horses. And there's not enough space to get them out quickly. Each chariot needs its own small area to allow for a wheel turn.'

The Commander looked between the two of them. 'What do you propose?'

Katep smoothed a place in the sand, took up a stick and began drawing. There was just enough moonlight for Anoukhet and me to make out what he was sketching. 'If this is the river and here's the cliff-face, we should gather hidden behind the cliffs and then come around on either side in a pincer movement, our bows at the ready. Without the chariots and the chariot runners charging our lines, we'll quickly take the upper hand and control the battle. But the big element for success must be surprise.'

The Commander glanced around at the assembled men. 'We mustn't waste a moment then. We must attack now!'

We watched as the meeting broke up and the men went to address their troops. Katep went between the soldiers of his phalanx and began to hiss out instructions and words of encouragement. 'Keep your voices down! Make yourself ready! Our weapon is surprise! Strength to you!' There was a brittle edge to his voice but I knew this was the moment he had been waiting for.

I hurried across the camp to help Kha hand out arrows. Not all the soldiers were as brave as I imagined. Some came forward with their faces pale in the moonlight and I heard quick incantations and, from some sides, even the sound of retching.

When Tuthmosis came for his arrows, I wanted to

hold them back from him and plead with him not to go. But I forced myself to say the words he needed to hear. 'This is your chance. Let Wosret know your strength! May the Lioness Sekhmet fight at your side.'

He held me against him hurriedly. For a moment his lips crushed mine but it was more with desperation than with passion. I could tell his head was already somewhere else. 'Keep safe!' was all he said as I clung to him.

When Anoukhet came, she thrust Kyky into my arms. 'Look after her.'

'What? Are you going?'

'Why else have I trained?'

'Wait for me, then.' But she was gone before I had a chance to gather my things. And by the time the arrows were all handed out, the camp was almost deserted.

'I can't stay, Kha. I have to join them. Look after Kyky for me.'

'A battlefield is no place for a girl!'

'Anoukhet's gone. You've always said an archer's only as good as his bow and arrow. If you made the bow and I made the arrow – what more could I need?'

He kissed my forehead. 'Take care then and be

sure to come back and fetch this monkey from me afterwards.'

The troops were already far ahead. I could just make out the dark massed shadow of them crawling over the distant sand dune in absolute silence, their shields moving like the plates on a giant armadillo. We had timed it well. Hathor was on our side. She had pulled her moon-eye from the sky. It was the dark time that comes just before dawn.

The sand dragged heavily at my boots as I struggled to catch up. The burden of the bow and the quiver full of arrows seemed to weigh me down. I'd forgotten to bring a water-skin and already my throat felt parched. I longed for a sip of palm wine now to still my thumping heart.

It was strange and unnerving being out in the desert on my own. A mist was sweeping up from the river. Wreaths of it hung low, hugging the dunes and lying in the valleys. I lost sight of the Nubian soldiers, as they carried no torches. But from the stars showing between the mist I knew the direction to take and once amongst the bowmen, I knew I would catch up with Anoukhet and Tuthmosis.

When I saw figures approaching, I imagined it to be my friends come looking for me. But something about their outlines as they came forward through the mist, made me change my mind. I began to run in the opposite direction.

'Halt!' I heard a rough Egyptian voice call out. 'Hold up or we shoot.'

I wrenched my bow from my shoulder and turned to load my arrow. If I was fast enough, I could shoot before they had time to draw theirs. But before I had taken up my stance, I heard the unmistakable whisper of a feathered arrow in full flight. With no time to steady my hands, I pulled back the sinew with all my strength and let my arrow fly in return. The kick of the bow ripped me in the chest and knocked me flat to the ground.

But the kick was not from my bow. It was from an arrow. It had hit me just above my collar bone. I felt around the shaft. My hands came away sticky with blood. A wave of nausea swept over me. The arrowhead needed to come out quickly. I clasped the shaft and, willing my hands to stop trembling, clenched my jaw, waiting for the rip and tear of flesh as I pulled, thinking I would die from the pain. Perhaps this was a flint arrowhead – perhaps I would *never* pull it free . . .

But I felt nothing. The arrow was not embedded. My moonstone amulet had blocked the full impact of its entry. The tip had lodged in my cloak and scarcely grazed the surface of my skin.

Before I had time to feel relief, I was surrounded by three soldiers. They seemed more boys than men. One shoved his foot against my chest and pinned me to the ground. 'Hold your swords, men! Before we kill the Kushite spy, let's find out what he knows.'

My mind was racing. How could I save myself? How could I turn this to my advantage? I struggled to find the right words. 'I'm *not* Kush. I'm Egyptian – like you.'

'Not Kush, eh?' He bent down and jerked my chin around towards the dawn light that was beginning to break and looked hard into my face. 'You have Egyptian features – but you're too dark.'

'I've been in the desert a long time. The sun has burned me.'

'Hah! And what would a lone Egyptian be doing so far from Egypt here among the Kush?'

I bit my lip, trying to think of the right response. 'You might well ask.'

'You mean you were captured by the Kush? Or are you an Egyptian deserter?'

I was silent while I tried desperately to decide what to answer.

'Which is it?' One of the boys grabbed me by the shoulder and wrenched me upright. In doing so he ripped open my cloak. He stared down. 'What? A girl!'

I grabbed the cloth and clutched it over my chest again.

He pushed his pimply face close to mine. Then he laughed as he glanced around at the others. 'An Egyptian girl! And quite a comely girl, at that! What are you doing amongst the Kush? A girl in soldiers' territory? A whore for Kushite soldiers? Is that what it is, eh?'

I shook my head. 'No! No, it isn't so!'

'Who's to believe you? It's your word against ours.' He turned to the others. 'What do you think, men?'

I tried to duck away but his hand gripped my shoulders all the harder.

'Perhaps she can be a whore for Egyptian soldiers now. It's only fair!'

Suddenly he lunged forward and, twisting one of my arms behind my back, began ripping at my tunic with his free hand. I squirmed and struggled to keep myself away from him. 'No, stop! Please! It's not what you think. You don't understand.'

'Yes, I do. I've known girls like you. Who like to

squeal and tease.' He thrust me onto the ground again and pinned me down. 'You can scream all you want. There's no one but us to hear you!'

He pressed his body close against me and fumbled with my clothes as he slobbered his mouth against my lips. I smelled the fumes of wine and the stink of onions and goat's meat on his breath. Then I reached back with my free hand and with all the strength I had, I thrust my fingers at his pimply face. Thrust as hard as I could. A short sharp jab that found the jelly of his eyes.

He sprang back in rage, clutching his face. 'She's blinded me! The whore has blinded me!'

Another soldier laughed as he bent forward to pull me up. 'She's not blinded you! But if she had it would serve you right for behaving like a goat! This girl's got more to tell than you think. She's no whore. She's a soldier. She carries a Kushite bow and Kushite arrows. An Egyptian, carrying Kushite weapons, must have a story to tell.'

I shook my head. My success had fuelled my anger. 'No!' I spat out. 'You mistake me. I'm *not* a soldier. I'm a spy working on the Egyptian side, dressed to look like a Kushite to blend with them. So I won't be recognised.'

276

He shook his head. 'The Egyptian army does not employ girl spies. And *if* by some chance it does, then you will not mind being taken back to the Egyptian camp to tell your story. If it *doesn't*, and you're a traitor ... then, how fortunate! Girls speak easily when under torture.' He turned to the others. 'Hold your spears. We'll take her back to camp.'

CHAPTER TWENTY-FIVE

SEKHMET ... LIONESS OF WAR

I was dragged down the dune by the men and led into their camp between Egyptian soldiers lying on the ground, who grumbled and cursed at us for disturbing their sleep. But before there was any chance of questioning me, shouts and bellows and more curses rang out from all directions.

'We're under attack!'

'Quick! Get the horses harnessed. Move the chariots out. Hurry to it!'

'It's the Kushites!'

Within moments soldiers were stumbling about, grabbing their weapons as arrows flew through the air, finding their mark all around us. Men shouted commands as others clutched wounds. Horses were rearing and plunging, donkeys braying, charioteers cracking whips, harnessing what horses they could and grabbing their bowmen on the run, hoisting them up alongside them and at the same time trying to turn their carts as men fell below the horses' hooves and were trampled.

In the pandemonium, I realised I had lost my captors and was loose in the crowd. I ducked low, using the crush of struggling men as cover, and scrambled to find my way out between their legs – trying to avoid the flaying hooves and trampling boots; trying not to be dragged down and to fall underfoot and at the same time struggling to keep under cover from the relentless hail of arrows which I knew by their colours were coming from Katep's men.

Hold up, Katep! Hold up! I prayed. I'm here, amongst them! But how was he to know?

Suddenly I was wrenched by my arm and swept up onto the platform of a passing chariot. The charioteer clutched me to him and held me behind his shield. I turned to thank my saviour. But I need not have bothered. He was the most evil-looking soldier I had ever seen, with wild eyes and a maniacal laugh. The disarray of the battle had thrown him into a frenzy. He had recognised my Kushite tunic. I wasn't being protected. I was being saved for something more important.

He let out a shriek of laughter at my terror. 'You want a battle! I'll give you a battle! You think your men are good bowmen. Well, let's see how accurate your archers can be with you as their target!'

He flung me across the front rail of the chariot and held me by my waist so that my legs dangled freely in the air above the wildly spinning wheels and the horses' rearing and plunging through the men. He whooped and cheered as he wheeled the horses around and at the same time took shelter behind me, using me as his shield, while his archer took shots over my shoulder at the approaching mass of Kush bowmen.

A cacophony of howls, shrieks and horses' whinnying rose up. The dawn was dark with arrows and the air around my ears whined with their passage. It was hard to know from which direction they came.

Then suddenly we galloped free from the throng of struggling Egyptian foot soldiers and were out in the open with nothing but an empty space between our chariot and the bowmen of Kush.

The chariot ran at full tilt towards them. With the

spittle of the horses flying back at me and the man's maniacal shouts in my ear, I made out row upon row of Kushite soldiers with arrows drawn, shields strapped to their arms, marching without falter towards us in a solid, unbroken mass.

I was going to die ... killed by the arrows of the Kush. There was no saving me now.

A dark cloud of arrows came straight at the chariot. I flailed and tried to wrench myself free and screamed out in blind panic, 'Hold your arrows. It's me. The fletcher! Don't shoot!' But there was no getting away from the Egyptian's grip and in the noise of battle it was hopeless. No one heard me.

I thought he would gallop his chariot into the midst of them. But he was too clever for that. Up close, swords would be drawn and the Kushites would have wrestled me free once they realised it was me. Instead, his triumph was to stay just out of their reach and to canter up and down in front of their line, holding me up and taunting them with his human shield.

I prayed to Hathor, Protector of Women, for mercy. I prayed to Sekhmet, Lioness of War, to strike him down. I prayed that Katep or Tuthmosis or Anoukhet or *someone* amongst the Kush would recognise me.

As if in answer, in the midst of the noise and disarray, a shout rang out.

'Hold up!' It was a woman's voice.

The rain of arrows from the Kushite bowmen stopped abruptly, as if choked by the unexpected shrillness of the sound.

A moment of utter silence followed. Then the whisper of a single, spinning arrow passed my face. I heard a thud behind me. A thud as dull as a boulder landing in thick river mud, followed instantly by a single intake of breath. The same sucking sound that mud makes when it accepts something heavy.

I turned. The arrow had taken the Egyptian high in the centre of his chest. It was an arrow with green feathers and shreds of red ribbon.

The man's sudden bellow shook both sides into action again. Arrows fell once more all around us. As the battle raged, the Egyptian clutched wildly at my body, still holding me up against the arrows. I felt the warmth of his blood seep against my back. My own hands came away sticky as I struggled to pull free of him. His blood? Or mine?

I caught the blurred movement of Anoukhet rushing forward. She sprang wildly past the horses and leaped towards the cart of the chariot, trying to hold onto the railing and at the same time grapple me from the Egyptian's grip.

The chariot was suddenly surrounded by Kushite bowmen. In the confusion I heard the metal slurring of swords being drawn. But before we could leap from the cart into the safety and protection of the Kushite throng, the Egyptian archer grabbed the reins from the slumped charioteer and wheeled the horses around so fast that the nearest Kushite swordsmen fell under their rearing hooves. Then he galloped the veering horses at full speed back towards the Egyptian side.

Anoukhet grabbed my arm. 'Quick! Jump!' she commanded. 'Jump! This is our only chance!'

But my legs went numb. The spinning spokes of the wheels and the thundering hooves turned my knees to water. I was incapable of standing upright, let alone jumping. In a blur of movement the chariot gained the other side and the Egyptian army closed ranks around us. We were dragged off and passed roughly over the soldiers' heads like bags of durum wheat being tossed from the hold of a ship and with as little care. Finally we were flung down on the ground, our hands wrenched behind us and, although we struggled and fought and bit at our captors, we weren't freed.

Instead we were dragged before a stake and tied back to back seated on either side of it, our arms pinned and trussed tightly against our bodies.

'Be brave,' Anoukhet whispered as she tried to reach backwards for my hand. 'Katep and Tuthmosis will come for us. They know we're here. That's why they've let up their arrows.'

Amidst the commotion and confusion of horses and men and chariots around us, I listened and knew she was right. The hail of arrows had stopped. But for how long? The Kushites wouldn't care about Anoukhet and me. They were hardened soldiers. They wouldn't stop their battle just for the likes of us.

'Vixens!' an Egyptian soldier hissed at us. 'We show no more mercy to women soldiers than we do to men!' He drew a khopesh from his girdle.

Anoukhet spat into the sand at his feet. I cringed and ducked my head as I imagined the dull blow to her neck.

Another soldier stepped forward. 'Wait!'

I could see by his cloak and gold broad-collar that he was a man of rank. He nodded his broad brutish face in our direction. 'They're bargaining tools. Not to be killed outright, but punished rather! To use as an example. So the Kushites will appreciate the strength

284

of the Egyptian army – and know we won't be trifled with.'

He came closer and glared down at Anoukhet. 'It was *your* arrow that killed our best charioteer? You found his heart, Kushite bitch!' Then he turned to a soldier at his side. 'Cut off her bow fingers – so she'll no longer know the accuracy of her draw. Take them off well. Make sure the dagger is sharp.'

I felt all blood drain from me and cringed as two men grabbed hold of Anoukhet's right hand and spread her fingers wide against the ground and pinned them down. I twisted my head from side to side looking for a glimpse of Katep or Tuthmosis. But my view was blocked by the soldiers shouting and jeering at our discomfort.

'Take her bow fingers! Take her bow fingers!'

I fought an urge to vomit. 'No! Don't!' I bellowed and twisted and tried to pull free. 'Take mine . . . not hers!'

The man with the gold collar looked down at me. 'Why not, my lovely? Is she your loved one that you would not have her scarred?'

'No! But she's not a bowman. Examine her hands. She has no callouses. She's *hopeless* with a bow. Her bow fingers are of no consequence.'

285

'If that's the case, she won't mind losing them. But you lie. I know differently. She shot my charioteer. She carried a bow when she was caught. A very fine bow at that. With very fine arrows. So she *is* a bowman.'

'By the truth of the white feather of Maat, how can you be sure it was her? There were Kushite bowmen everywhere.'

'What? You have the audacity to swear by Egyptian gods?'

'The gods do not belong to Egypt!'

'You're Egyptian – yet a *traitor* to all that is Egyptian.' He turned to a soldier. 'Take hers as well!' Then he kicked at me with his foot. 'And be glad your punishment is mild! When last the Egyptian army, under the Great Amenhotep, fought Nubia, we took seven-hundred and forty able-bodied prisoners and from the fallen we cut not just fingers, but three-hundred and twenty hands as punishment.'

'What?' I spat at him. 'Only three-hundred and twenty hands! How pale a victory!'

He turned abruptly to the soldier. 'Curse these women for their audacity! Yes, take hers as well. Teach them both a lesson. Take their bow fingers, now! I command it!'

A murmur went up. 'Yes! Yes!'

'Take the bow fingers! The bow fingers!'

'The loss of two fingers is nothing to me!' I spat out. 'I could as easily learn to draw a bow with my left hand.' I stared at them unflinchingly while they hesitated, trying to win time for Anoukhet. My blood was pulsing hot and angry now. If I had not been tied, I would have attacked them with my fists. 'Take all my fingers! Take my hands, for all I care! That's if you have the stomach for it . . . cowards!'

'No! No!' Anoukhet begged as she groped for my hand. 'Don't taunt them, Kara! They'll do it! I know the campaign they speak of.'

But before she could say more, the soldiers bent forward and spread her fingers again. I felt my throat constrict. Felt the words shrivel on my tongue. Then everything turned soundless. As if my ears were blocked. Yet I knew there was noise all around me.

The dagger came down swiftly. I squeezed my eyes shut so as not to witness it find its mark – but not fast enough to stop me from seeing the spray of Anoukhet's blood that fanned out across the sand.

And then, they took the first two fingers of my own right hand as well.

287

CHAPTER TWENTY-SIX

TUTHMOSIS

Afterwards it seemed a blur. What actions came in which order is hard to sort out in my mind. My head was so dizzy I thought I would faint.

I remember the blind, numb pain and my body shaking. I remember the vague outline of the man in the gold broad-collar standing over us as we sat slumped together against the post. Coward! I wanted to shout – to be so set on maiming two girls. It's victory for *us* that you felt the need to cut off our bow fingers. It's victory for *us* that you have sunk so low! We have more bravery in the fingers you've sliced off, than you have in your *whole body*!

But my mouth wouldn't form around the words.

Whether I spoke them aloud or not, I can't be sure.

A sudden swell of voices roused me.

'Victory is Egypt's!'

'The Kushites have ceased their fight! They've given up!'

Cheers broke out. Men beat their swords against their shields. The earth shook with the stamp of hundreds of feet. 'Vic – tory! Vic – tory! Vic – tory!' came the chant.

'Given up? They can't have!' I twisted around to look at Anoukhet. 'This is all my doing. It's because I was captured. They've lost the battle because of me!'

'*Never!*' She hissed back at me. 'They would never give up!'

A soldier pointed at us. 'What about them, Captain?'

'Load them on that chariot and display them to the Kushites to show how easily a battle is won when women are made soldiers.'

'The battle is *not* over!' Anoukhet bellowed. 'The Kushites would *never* cease to fight!' I felt her struggling to free herself at my back. 'Cut these ropes. I'll go to them and tell them what cowards the Egyptian army are, that you hide behind chariots and horses with women as your shields while the Kushites fight out in the open, shoulder to shoulder as one man. Free me so I can return to battle. I will use my other arm!'

There was raucous laughter. 'She's a wildcat! A real vixen!'

The man they called Captain walked across and crouched down next to her.

I strained my neck to see Anoukhet's face, but kept my eyes averted from her hand and mine.

He gripped her under her jaw and lifted her head so that she was incapable of looking anywhere but directly back at him. A horrible sneer was etched across his brutish face. 'And then? What then, my lovely?'

'You'll be the first to die by my arrow!' Anoukhet spat out.

He studied her seriously. Then shook his head. 'I think not! Do you believe I'm troubled by the threat of a slave girl? We'll capture you again. And then, my lovely, it's not just your bow fingers we'll cut off. We'll dismember you bit by slow bit, until you beg us to stop. And your bowmen will be ridden down like dogs under our horses' hooves.' He flung her jaw away from him and stood up abruptly. '*Then* let's see your Kushites come grovelling and begging us for mercy.'

'Never!'

'Don't you see they've deserted both of you? Don't you see what cowardly dogs they've proved to be, retreating and leaving two women to our mercy?'

'Mercy? Hah! When did an Egyptian soldier *ever* show mercy? Is cutting off a finger mercy?'

Without warning, an arrow whistled through the air and flew down at an angle, pinning the toe of the Captain's left boot to the ground. Then another came in quick succession, and shivered to a halt in the toe of his other boot. The arrows had bright red feathers without a pattern.

Despite the searing pain of my hand, I felt a smile creep across my face at the silly sight of this man pinned down with two red-feathered arrows sticking up from his toes. I twisted around to see from which direction the arrows had come, searching for a sign of Katep.

Then his voice shouted down from the cliffs. 'The Kushites have retreated by my Commander's orders. Look to the top of this cliff and you'll see five hundred arrows pointed directly at you and your men – each one marking the heart of his individual target. The Commander has only to give the order and they'll be released. Each arrow will find an Egyptian heart.'

The Captain's eyes flashed with anger as he searched the cliff for Katep. Then he wrenched his feet free of the two arrows. 'Hah! From such an angle and from so far, you'll not find your target,' he bellowed. 'You've not even found my foot!'

'I could find the mole on your cheek. We are the People of the Bow. There are no better marksmen on this earth.'

'Be brave enough to show yourself, then.'

There was a movement to my side and I saw an Egyptian soldier very slowly and stealthily lift his bow.

'Show yourself!' the Captain taunted again.

'No! Katep! Don't!' I bellowed.

A dagger was suddenly at my throat, pressing hard up against my skin with its sharp tip. 'Silence!' the Captain hissed next to my ear.

From the corner of my eye I saw a figure suddenly appear on the cliff. It wasn't Katep but Tuthmosis. He stood above us totally transformed. He had found a leopard cloak. It hung from his shoulder and wrapped his body with its great claws. Even from a distance I could see the gold pectoral shining against his chest. And on his head he wore the single tall white ostrich plume of Truth. He carried no weapons.

'Let her go!' he commanded.

The Captain glanced upwards. 'So you are Katep! What is it to you if I don't?'

'I'm not Katep.'

The Captain gripped me harder. His arm was choking me. I felt a small trickle run down my neck. Sweat or blood – I wasn't sure.

'Who are you to order a Captain of the Egyptian army? You have no authority over me!'

'Do as I say!'

'What is she to you? What will you do to save her life?' he sneered.

I felt the blood hammer behind my eyes as I struggled to breathe. One thrust and the dagger would slice through my throat. One sharp jerk of the man's arm and my neck would be broken. There was silence. Everyone focused on Tuthmosis and waited for his answer.

'I don't have to bargain. I am Tuthmosis, son of Amenhotep. By my authority as King, I order you to let her go.'

'*King?*' The Captain began to laugh as he released his grip. I slumped back against the post.

'Do you hear that? This piece of dirt thinks he is the son of the great Amenhotep!' He looked around at the group of soldiers, then threw back his head and laughed even louder.

With the speed of the leopard he wore, Tuthmosis jumped from the ledge right at the Captain. They sprawled to the ground. The Captain was taken completely by surprise and, before anyone had a chance to react, Tuthmosis had wrestled the dagger away from him. Then, with one stride and a quick upward thrust, he sliced through the rope that bound both Anoukhet and me and eased us to our feet. I stood trembling, feeling I would vomit. Next to me Anoukhet was silent.

Then I heard the soft swish of bows being lifted. Whether it came from the Egyptians or the Kushites on the cliffs, I wasn't sure. My body stiffened.

Tuthmosis stepped in front of us and addressed the Egyptians. 'You may draw your arrows but the Kushites on these cliffs are quicker. It's true what has been said. You each have an arrow aimed at your heart.'

For a moment there was complete silence as each side waited.

'You will regret this day!' the Captain warned.

Tuthmosis held up the heavy gold pectoral that hung across his chest. The carnelian and lapis lazuli caught the rays of the rising sun and glinted. But it was the huge central stone of the scarab that seemed like a living green light of fire. It sparked and flashed in every direction, invoking the power of the gods.

'This is the pectoral insignia of my heritage. It bears my name.' Tuthmosis's voice echoed around the cliffs and must have been heard by even the furthest soldier. 'By this I'm the King's son. Appointed by the gods to rule Egypt. I am the intermediary that stands between the gods and you – the people of Egypt. If you harm me, you harm the gods. Their wrath will come down on you, and your families, and Egypt, a hundredfold.'

I sensed rather than saw the Egyptians around me drop their bows. A soldier next to me clutched an amulet at his throat and another drew a wedjat eye in the sand with the tip of his boot.

'The God of Chaos will come down on you. I will put the curse of—'

I heard the soldiers gasp and call out to prevent Tuthmosis from speaking the name of the God of Chaos.

'Hah!' the Captain spat out. 'So it's true! You *are* Tuthmosis! It's true what Wosret said! You hide here amongst the Kushites. A coward! A traitor turned *against* Egypt. Then you have the audacity to call on

Egyptian gods. Your brother has been appointed by
the High Priests of Thebes as King. *He* is the living
God – not *you*! You have *no* power over us! The gods
will not listen to you!'

'Kill him, Tuthmosis!' Anoukhet hissed. 'He's
insulted you! If you don't, I must.' She pushed
forward and with her left hand tried to grapple the
knife away from Tuthmosis.

'Be still, Anoukhet!' He gripped her arm tightly. 'I
don't need his blood on my hands. It's honour I want
– not blood! There must be no more bloodshed.'

Anoukhet tossed her head and thrust her shoulders
back defiantly. 'This is what we fought for,' she hissed.

For a moment the two of them stared at one another
with blazing eyes. Then Tuthmosis turned. I saw him
take in the scene of the bodies of the dead soldiers
that lay around us. 'No!' he shook his head. 'Look
around you. This is *not* what we fought for. Does
Egypt stand for this? Bloody battle after bloody battle?
Men slaughtered because of the need and avarice of a
few? My father was a leader who willed people to die
for him. Is this what makes a good king?'

'Your father was a brave man!' the Captain hissed.
'But you're nothing but a coward!'

Tuthmosis turned to him with slate-hard eyes.

'I won't kill you. But take this message back to Wosret. Say the Kingdom of Egypt belongs to my brother. But tell him that should he *ever* send his army south again to attack the Kushites and to lay claim to their land and possessions, by this pectoral I will return to take my rightful throne.'

'*What?*' Anoukhet grabbed his arm with her uninjured hand. 'No, Tuthmosis . . . you can't do this! You have to take it *now*! We came all this way for you to fight for your Kingdom. Now it's yours! Kill this man and be done with it. He's nothing but a poisonous viper. Stand up for yourself. Let them see you are Tuthmosis – King of Egypt!'

From the corner of my eye I saw the quick movement the Captain made. He grabbed a khopesh from a soldier. I saw it glint in the sunlight. Then he swung it back with all his might. But just as the blade came slicing in an arc to find its mark against Anoukhet's neck and silence her once and for all, his feet staggered from beneath him, his arm flailed wide and the khopesh flew out of his hand.

He fell prone at our feet. Protruding from his chest was one of Katep's red arrows.

And then, as if this was a sign, a hail of arrows pelted down from the cliff. They darkened the sky as thick as a swarm of locusts and found their mark around us.

'Quick!' Tuthmosis grabbed hold of Anoukhet and me and dragged us to the nearest chariot. 'Leap on! Hurry! The battle has begun. The Kushite bowmen have run out of patience. We can't stay them any longer. Take up any weapon you find. We'll fight our way through the Egyptians.'

He snatched up the reins and wheeled the horses around so that the sand spun up in our faces and the chariot plunged forward between arrows flying in all directions.

'Hold on well!' he shouted, as soldiers tried to pull the horses down. 'And pray the wheels are made of strong wood and the axel and linchpins hold.'

Then, as we broke free, he grinned back at us with his leopard cloak flying and its paws clawing the wind and laughed as he saw our faces. 'And be glad this is not the first time I've driven a chariot!'

CHAPTER TWENTY-SEVEN

ON THE BANK OF THE GREAT RIVER IN THE LAND OF KUSH

Later that day we sat on the bank of the river in silence, Anoukhet and I each with thick bandages around our throbbing hands. We had drunk the herbal mixture the old man Kha had brewed for us before he stitched our wounds closed with a horn needle. And we had used the bee-sting ointment made by him to reduce the swelling and pain but, despite the numbness, my hand still throbbed.

Behind us the desert had turned to shimmering gold. Anoukhet squinted into the late afternoon sun. Then she looked directly at Katep. 'I can't understand it! Why did you wait so long to kill the Egyptian Captain?'

'I killed him in the end.'

'But only afterwards.' She narrowed her eyes at him. I knew her well enough. She was seething with anger. 'Why did you shoot at his feet first? He was worse than a horned viper. He didn't deserve the chance to live.'

Katep shook his head. 'You don't understand. When I pinned his feet, I wasn't giving *him* the chance to live. I was giving *you and Kara* the chance to live.'

'How so?'

'I couldn't risk killing him while the two of you were tied up. The moment we killed him, his soldiers would've slaughtered you.'

'You said you had arrows aimed at their hearts. Why didn't you carry out your threat and kill them all? Why did you wait?'

I saw Tuthmosis look up and exchange glances with Katep. 'Because I asked him not to.'

Anoukhet sat forward sharply and stared at him. 'What? This was a battle! The People of the Bow had their arrows trained on the soldiers of the Egyptian army – who had come south to vanquish them and capture you! This was your chance, Tuthmosis, to defeat Egypt with the whole Kush army behind you. Your chance to show Wosret your power.'

Tuthmosis seemed to have lost interest in the conversation. He scratched in the sand with the tip of a reed across the pathway of a shiny-green metallic beetle.

'Why did you stop Katep from giving the command to kill them all?' She turned her blazing eyes on Katep. 'And why did you listen to him?'

'Because Tuthmosis is the rightful King of Egypt.'

'He's not *your* King! You've become a Kushite now. You don't have to take orders from an *Egyptian*! Least of all someone who doesn't stand up for his rights!'

Tuthmosis glanced up. 'I didn't *order* him. I *asked* him not to shoot.'

'But why?'

'For the same reason I gave up my throne.'

Anoukhet jumped up abruptly and looked down at him through narrow slit eyes. 'It makes no sense!'

Katep reached out and tried to pull her down next to him. 'That's because you're a fighter.'

She snatched her arm away as if his touch had hurt her. 'What's wrong with being a fighter?'

'There's nothing wrong with it. You fight to stay free and true to yourself. Unfettered and unthwarted. It's what makes you strong! It's not easy to stay true to yourself. It was the reason I left Thebes.'

Anoukhet looked back at him with fiery eyes. 'You haven't stayed true to yourself! You let Tuthmosis overrule you with his princely ideas that have no meaning or place on a battlefield!'

'That's unfair, Anoukhet!' Blood was pulsing at my temples and I felt my left hand clench. I was ready to do battle and defend Katep. Or was it Tuthmosis I was defending? It was so confusing. I stared from one to the other as Anoukhet glared back at us. Around us the afternoon was filled with the sharp cry of waterfowl and the discordant croaking of frogs.

It felt as if all the air had been punched from my lungs. 'Why are we fighting? The Kushites proved themselves. They stood up to the power of Egypt and beat them back. The Egyptians have scuttled back to their boats as hurriedly as cockroaches looking for cover. And we weren't captured. Right now we could've been prisoners, marching back to Thebes. But we aren't. We should be celebrating, not fighting amongst ourselves!'

Anoukhet scowled across at me and then at Tuthmosis. 'No! we can't celebrate! Not until Tuthmosis tells us why he gave up his right.'

Tuthmosis stared back at her. 'Why did you and Kara sacrifice your bow fingers?'

'We had no choice!'

He shook his head. 'That's not what I'm asking. I'm asking – why did you go into battle? What were your reasons?'

'You know the answer. We fought for you. We wanted justice done for you.'

'I wanted justice as well. But many people suffered and died in that battle.'

'Then why did you give up so easily?' she spat out. 'Their deaths and our injuries stand for nothing now! You let the Kushites down. You let us *all* down!' She stamped her foot in the sand as if she wanted to rid herself of the thought. 'Why? Why did you do it?'

'I stood on the cliff and looked down and was sickened by what I saw. There were bodies lying everywhere. The Egyptian soldiers were fighting under orders, believing they were fighting for the good of Egypt.'

'But that's what soldiers *do*,' Anoukhet snapped back at him.

'Yes, but I realised that to be King, I'd have to spend the rest of my life in battle . . . always plotting and vanquishing. In that system, the only way to fight fire *is* with fire. I'd have to send men to war, not

303

because *they* wanted to do battle but because of *my* desire to stay in power. I'd have to plot and counter-plot to keep ahead. To wrest and wrench my power from everyone around me like a hunter wringing all life from a waterfowl. As ruthless in my ways as Wosret.'

Anoukhet narrowed her eyes, but said nothing.

He broke a tiny piece from his reed and balanced it across the back of the beetle. 'It's simple. Think of this beetle. If I pack too much on its back, it won't be able to move across the sand. When you're too greedy, you fail. The goal of our quest was to grab back power. But when I looked around me, I realised that to grab back power by violence is not a noble quest.'

'It's what Egypt has always done! She's vanquished all the lands around her for their wealth.'

'That doesn't make it right. You can't fight violence with more violence. That sort of power corrupts. I don't want to be an overlord recognised not for my dignity, but for the power of my chariots and sword. No power can be good when it comes at the expense of others.'

Anoukhet whipped around. 'Hah! When did you decide *that*?'

'When I saw you and Kara have your fingers taken. I vowed then. I held my pectoral in my hand and looked at the heart scarab, and I knew.'

'Knew what?'

He shrugged. 'A stone heart is just that – a stone heart – whether it's of lapis lazuli or emerald. It's not the real heart. It's only a symbol – like any amulet placed in mummy wrappings to prevent the real heart being stolen from the body.'

There was silence as Anoukhet sized him up. Then her words came out like sparks spitting from a fire. 'So you gave it all up! Our sacrifice was for nothing! We lost our bow fingers. You lost your Kingdom.' She snapped her thumb against the fingers of her left hand. 'Just like that! All because you had a change of heart.'

Katep pressed his hands against her shoulders to calm her. 'You can't say the sacrifice was worthless. We each came to Nubia searching for something more.'

'Like what?' she rasped.

'Freedom, perhaps?'

I looked around at their faces. Something was nagging at me. I thought of my father's honour and the stories Wosret must have spread. And I thought of

Naqada. I felt uneasy, as if something was pressing against my chest, squeezing air from my lungs. Perhaps, to be finally free of the burden of Naqada, I'd have to tell my secret to Katep.

I looked across at him and took a deep breath. 'Can you find freedom when you've killed someone?'

Katep glanced back at me without saying anything. 'Why do you ask?'

'I've killed a man.'

I expected to see a startled look in his eyes. But he just nodded. 'I know. Anoukhet told me. You protected her. We've each killed for the love of one another.'

Tuthmosis looked across at me. Then he laughed as if to break the tension. Suddenly he picked up the beetle and held it towards me in the cup of his hand. 'Here . . . I won't give you my pectoral with its stone heart, I'll give you my real heart in the form of this living scarab.'

'Your heart?'

He shrugged as his eyes held mine, blue and intense as the colour of the sky. 'It's much more alive than the heart of any emerald.'

I sensed the other two watching us. 'Don't tease, Tuthmosis.'

306

'I'm not teasing.'

'But ...?' I couldn't find the right words. I felt myself blushing. Perhaps I had misunderstood what he was saying. 'I thought ...' Yes, I'd definitely misunderstood.

He was looking at me with a broad smile now. 'Haven't we found freedom? Hasn't it been because of you that I have the courage to be free now?'

'Me?'

'Your bravery has made me brave.'

'Kiss her then, silly!' Anoukhet was suddenly grinning. 'So she knows how you feel!'

And he did. He bent forward and placed his lips against mine and held me so close and kissed me for so long, I thought I'd stop breathing.

When he finally released me, Anoukhet started to laugh. 'Listen to the frogs. It's a marriage party. There'll be masses of tadpoles afterwards to bestow eternal life.'

Frogs? A thought came to me. Everything was falling into place. I jumped up. 'Wait! I've just remembered something. A frog and a scarab beetle.'

'What?' They looked at me strangely.

'I know the secret of the Senet board! Don't you see?' I fumbled in my girdle pouch and took out my

307

father's Senet board and moved closer. 'Look, there's a frog and a scarab etched into the squares on the board.'

Anoukhet clicked her tongue. 'There are almost as many frogs and scarabs as there are grains of sand in Egypt and Nubia!'

'No, look again. Look at the other symbols. Think of the journey we've made.' I glanced at Tuthmosis. 'Remember in the labyrinth we found our way out because of the thirty turquoise tiles? We discovered the exit tile of Ra.'

They were staring blankly at me.

'Don't you see – my father was right! It's a game of passage. Except we've gone the other way around. We've travelled in the opposite direction.'

Tuthmosis shook his head. 'Opposite? What do you mean?'

'We weren't *exiting* at the Ra square. We were *starting* the journey. Entering our new life. Everything we've done since matches up with a marked tile on the board.' I held it up. 'There's the symbol of the net for the labyrinth, the wavy lines for the waters of chaos, even you are here, Katep, in the boat. See! Your outline is marked by stars. The hunter constellation, Orion.'

308

Katep smiled and shook his head. 'I thought it was just a game!'

Anoukhet eyed me. 'It *is* just a game. You said the turquoise tiles in the passageway were unmarked.'

I nodded. 'They were unmarked because our journey was unknown. We didn't know what was ahead.'

Tuthmosis's eyes met mine. He smiled. 'In a way we've made our own Senet board.'

'Yes. Every square is a stage in our lives. They're tests, whether you move backwards or forwards. We pass through labyrinths, get sucked into the waters of chaos along the way and call on the gods to rescue us. The symbols are different for each of us. Everyone does the journey in their own way.'

'You mean the symbol of the heart scarab means one thing to you and another to us?' Katep teased.

'You can mock, but the only thing that matters is that we made the journey.'

'Does that mean we've won?'

I smiled back at him. 'I suppose it does.'

Anoukhet caught me by the arm. 'So now? What next?'

I shrugged. 'To our freedom?'

Tuthmosis glanced between us. 'And perhaps a new game of Senet?'

'Yes! Yes – that's it!' Anoukhet laughed. She did a whirling dance around us with Kyky at her heels in the light that was turning soft and milky over the river as the sun dipped down. 'To freedom and new adventures!'

Katep reached out to catch her. 'Will you stay here in the Land of Kush?'

She stood still for a moment, and then tossed her head. 'Will you teach me to handle a bow and arrow with my left hand?'

'Yes!'

'Then I will!'

'And you, Kara? Will you stay?' Katep was watching my face. His glance seemed to polish the thin silver thread that I knew still ran between us.

I shrugged. 'I don't know yet.'

All three of us turned to Tuthmosis.

He shook his head. 'I can't stay. I must return to Thebes.'

'Why?' Anoukhet demanded.

'To face Wosret properly.'

'But you said you had given up!'

'I need to face him – not with a sword, but as a man. Justice needs to be done.'

*

Later, as the sun dropped below the horizon, Katep and Tuthmosis went back to the Kushite camp to help with the dismantling of it.

A full moon rose up over the river, huge and luminous, and sent a sheen of silver across the smooth water. In the glow that still lay in the west, a long skein of vaporous cloud turned turquoise. It floated like a fine, transparent robe along the horizon touched at one end with orange carnelian.

I turned to look at Anoukhet and saw her nod.

We had both seen her. It was Hathor, floating across the sky in her turquoise robe, with the moon resting gently on her head and the last sunlight flaring on the carnelian of her cobra earrings.

I found myself smiling. Her rearing cobras were nothing to be frightened of. They had been our protectors. They had spat their venom on our enemies. And now she had come to give Anoukhet and me her blessing. Hathor – Eye of Wisdom, Truth and Secrets; Protector of Women; Eye of the Moon.

I felt for my mother's moonstone at my throat and for the warmth of the cowrie shell and saw Anouhket touch hers as well.

'You'll leave us too, won't you?'

I nodded. 'I must. I can't remain in Nubia. The

honour of my father must be restored. The Temple of Sobek waits for me.'

'What?' Anoukhet raised an eyebrow. 'The Temple of Sobek? Do the crocodiles hold no fear for you?'

I picked up a flat pebble and held it awkwardly, weighing it up for size and smoothness – thinking about her question. Eventually the stone lay comfortable and calm in the cup of my left hand. Then I held it between my fingers, flicked back my wrist and threw it as hard as I could across the water. I held my breath – waiting for it to sink. But it jumped and skipped like a fish coming up for air. As good as any throw I had ever made.

I shook my head. 'Not any more! None at all!'

Anoukhet smiled broadly. Then she searched for a perfectly flat stone and with a swift flick of her left hand, sent it leaping after mine. 'Every time the moon is full I'll throw a pebble and know you'll be doing the same.'

I bartered for two pairs of earrings in the marketplace the next day. Nothing grand like carnelian, or turquoise or gold . . . but simple agate, carved crudely but well enough to see they are rising cobras. We both wear them dangling next to our faces now – constant protectors, guarding us through every moment until we meet again.

Now I sit here on the bank of the Great River on my journey back to Thebes, with Tuthmosis not far off hunting wildfold in the reeds. And I write as fast as my injured hand will let me of all that has happened since that morning when a shaving of moon came into the sky like a thread of spun flax, at the time of Queen Tiy's death. I write on papyrus but perhaps in time these words will be carved in stone and the truth known to all.

May anyone who reads them, know they are written by the feather of Truth, under the protection of the Eye of the Moon.

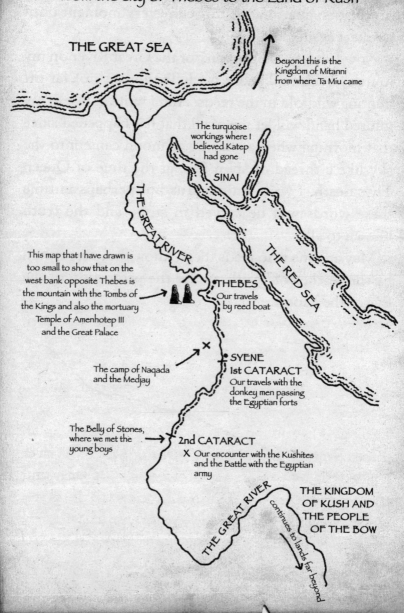

The route Tuthmosis and I took along the Great River from the city of Thebes to the Land of Kush

THE GREAT SEA

Beyond this is the Kingdom of Mitanni from where Ta Miu came

The turquoise workings where I believed Katep had gone

SINAI

THE GREAT RIVER

THE RED SEA

This map that I have drawn is too small to show that on the west bank opposite Thebes is the mountain with the Tombs of the Kings and also the mortuary Temple of Amenhotep III and the Great Palace

THEBES
Our travels by reed boat

The camp of Naqada and the Medjay

SYENE
1st CATARACT
Our travels with the donkey men passing the Egyptian forts

The Belly of Stones, where we met the young boys

2nd CATARACT
X Our encounter with the Kushites and the Battle with the Egyptian army

THE KINGDOM OF KUSH AND THE PEOPLE OF THE BOW

THE GREAT RIVER

continues to lands far beyond

AUTHOR'S NOTE

Two double-page spreads of three mutilated mummies splashed across a Sunday paper were the catalyst for this story. One of the mummies was believed to be the much-loved Queen Tiy, grandmother of Tutankhamen. Next to her lay a young boy with a severe leg injury and, next to him, a mummy that was possibly Nefertiti, beautiful wife of Tiy's second son, Amenhotep.

But why were the three mummies sealed up in a tiny insignificant chamber and why were they mutilated?

Murder, mystery and intrigue are part of the history of Egypt and for this story I've drawn on all these elements. Egyptology sleuths will soon discover I killed off Queen Tiy about ten years too early and allowed her elder son, Tuthmosis, to escape death. So while the main historical events are accurate, a few liberties have been taken and the city of Thebes has been called by its more commonly known name, rather than Waset, as it would have been then.

The fact that Egypt's magic is ever present, was shown me by some uncanny co-incidences. I had presumed the crippled leg of the boy to be a birth defect. But because he was to be the hero of my story, I invented a chariot accident. Later, I realised how close I had come to the possible truth when, in *The Search for Nefertiti*, Joann Fletcher observed after examining the boy mummy:

'I wondered if the family obsession with fast horses and chariot racing had had anything to do with the prince's horrific injury.'

Another strange moment came with the original title – *Eye of Horus*. The right eye of Horus represents Osiris and the sun. The left eye represents Isis and the moon. These are the Wedjat eyes and are always shown as being dark. Yet when I came to print out one, even though my black ink cartridge was full, for some mysterious reason, the eye appeared in the negative – white and slightly blue-flecked – exactly like a full moon.

I had found the perfect title . . . *Eye of the Moon*.

Dianne Hofmeyr